God rest ye merry, gentlemen.

"Hello," Jim said.

A muffled voice said, "Merry Christmas, Jimbo."

"Who is this?" Jim said.

"It's me, Brian," the voice said. "I just wanted to say Merry Christmas and tell you I sent you a gift. You'll find it in the glove compartment of your car. And you don't have to worry about opening it. It's not a bomb."

There was a click then and the line went dead.

So now Jim knew. Brian was alive. And Brian knew that he was after him.

It could be a Merry Christmas for only one of them—the one who got to the other first.

"The seductive virtue [of this novel] is a notably brilliant narrative method—tight, objective, cinematic, relentless, and irresistible. The story, of a deadly intercontinental duel between a betrayed agent and the traitor who all but destroyed him, is a good one; but it's the telling that makes it truly distinctive."—*The New York Times Book Review*

75¢

The
KILLING
SEASON

Adam Kennedy

A KANGAROO BOOK
PUBLISHED BY POCKET BOOKS NEW YORK

THE KILLING SEASON

Trident Press edition published 1967

POCKET BOOK edition published July, 1968

2nd printing.....................February, 1977

This POCKET BOOK edition includes every word contained in
the original, higher-priced edition. It is printed from brand-
new plates made from completely reset, clear, easy-to-read type.
POCKET BOOK editions are published by
POCKET BOOKS,
a division of Simon & Schuster, Inc.,
A GULF+WESTERN COMPANY
630 Fifth Avenue,
New York, N.Y. 10020.
Trademarks registered in the United States
and other countries.

FOR
Roy and Ann

part |

■ 1 ■

DAWN IN BERLIN. SILENT AND SOFT THE CITY BEGAN TO wake up. Quietly at first. Blankets folded back warm. Night clothes slipped to the floor. Soap and water lathered soundlessly together. Coffee steamed and kettles bubbled in thousands of silent kitchens.

Quiet. Even in the street. No horns sounded in the light traffic. No bells. And no voices raised. No anger yet. No blame and no denials.

Empty buses and streetcars rolled out of barns and garages. Roses and carnations and fresh-cut flowers glowed in the gray light as flower stands and flower carts came to life.

Sidewalks began to be hosed and swept now and milk was delivered. Policemen in white gloves arrived at traffic stations. Beef and lamb carcasses and long pink loins of pork and heavy hams were hefted and pushed onto trucks, unloaded and carried into restaurant kitchens. Bundles of newspapers thumped to the sidewalk in front of just opening kiosks. Cyclists rolled past with lunch pails in their strapped-on bicycle baskets.

In the neighborhood markets, vegetable and fruit bins filled and overflowed. Burlap bags of white-scrubbed potatoes and turnips and purple onions stood jammed in rows together. Peppers were strung and hung. Fishes gutted and iced. But no shoppers came yet. Not quite yet.

In the apartment buildings and in the private brick homes with their neatly walled or fenced foreyards and in the two-

9

family or three-family dwellings in Steglitz or Wittenau, many lights were on now.

The bathing and dressing and eating were well begun. Lovemaking resumed and old arguments flickered to new life in bedrooms and across kitchen tables.

Children were awake now and pets were being fed. Parrots and canaries came out from under their night coverings. And in the sidewalk bars, a few workmen stood like sections of tree trunks and lifted their steins or wine glasses.

The guard changed at all the crossover points along the wall. Simply and quietly. Monosyllabic.

The light was up stronger now. And the volume. More people on the buses and streetcars and crossing at intersections. And riding bicycles.

Hair combed, teeth brushed, eyes clear now or at least coming clear, voices accustomed to speech again, stomachs warmed with food or wine or coffee, the city opaque and intricate was coming full awake now.

From the side door of a red brick house on Koenigsallee, a nine-year-old boy ran out. He started to bounce a tennis ball against a wall behind his house and field it in the pocket of an American baseball glove autographed by Tony Kubek. Over and over he bounced the ball with a thwonking sound against the wall and caught it as it came back.

Jim Gallagher, age thirty-three, brindle-haired and gray-eyed, turned over in bed, burrowed his head into the pillow hollow and tried to shut out the sound of the ball bouncing against the bricks. After a moment or two, the sound going on relentlessly, he turned on his back and looked at the clock beside his bed. Ten minutes to six. He propped his head on the bunched-up pillow and lighted a cigarette.

Beside him his wife, Joan Okada Gallagher, also thirty-three, born in Salinas of Japanese parents, a delicate and lovely girl and a famously sound sleeper. Now, as her husband smoked beside her and as the neighbor child continued to bounce his ball, she slept soundly.

Several kilometers northeast, past the Reichstag and Congress Hall and the Hansa quarter, in a second-floor front apartment in a new apartment building on Perleberger Strasse, another young man lay fully dressed, hands clasped behind his head, on his bed. Brian Ramsey, age thirty-five, a British citizen born in Australia, raised in Manila, Hong Kong, and Liverpool. Clear blue-eyed and blond hair brushed back.

His face was peaceful, innocent and complete, all his questions answered. The lamp was on beside his bed but he wasn't reading or smoking or glancing at his watch. He simply waited.

Still further north and a bit to the east, in an older building on a quiet residential street off Schwedenstrasse, Burt Wager, age fifty-five, brown eyes and graying crew-cut hair, his face etched and grooved, crow's-footed and crosshatched, was typing a letter and drinking coffee. On the desk beside him was a framed photograph of a handsome, big-boned woman and two teen-age boys.

Gallagher stubbed out his cigarette now and eased himself out of the bed. Carefully and quietly. He stood up, tall, narrow, and well-knit. Straight-backed and long-legged. His face was brown and smooth, his cheeks sloping down flat from the jut of his cheekbones.

He strapped his watch on his wrist and picked up his robe from the back of a chair. As he pulled it on over his pajamas he walked to the window and looked down at the kid in the driveway. Unbroken rhythm. Throw, bounce, catch. Throw, bounce, catch.

Jim finished knotting the belt of his robe and moved away from the window toward the door. As he put his hand on the knob, Joannie opened her eyes and raised herself on one elbow. "Hey," she said, "you sneak."

"I thought you were asleep," Jim said. He eased the door closed again and moved back toward the bed.

"I was."

"Well, go back to sleep," he said. "It's early."

"Early, early, early," she said.

"Go on. Go back to sleep."

"Where are you going?" Joannie asked. He said he was getting up.

"Oh, please," she said. "Don't get up. Then I'll have to get up."

"No, you won't. Sleep, you rat." He sat down on the edge of the bed and pulled her over to him.

"I can't sleep by myself," she said. "You know that."

"I know that's what you always say."

"It's always true," she said. "What time is it?"

"A little after six. Seven minutes after."

"Oh, God," she said. And then, "I train my two kids from

11

infancy. I train them to sleep until seven o'clock. Then look what happens."

"We move next door to a shortstop," Jim said.

"They don't even *play* baseball in Germany."

"He does," Jim said.

"Come back to bed," Joannie said. She lay back down and pulled on Jim's hand.

"I thought you were sleepy," Jim said.

"I am," Joannie said. "Come on, Jimbo."

Jim nodded his head toward the window and said, "What's the use? He's still going at it."

"Come on," she said. "We'll put cotton in our ears."

"All right," he said. He stood up and walked to the door. "I'll be back in a minute."

"What now?"

"I'm going to look at the kids."

"Don't wake them up," she said.

"I won't."

Jim closed the door behind him and walked quietly down the hallway to the children's room. There he eased the door open and stepped inside. In the shades-drawn dim light of the room, he pulled the blankets up over Jake Gallagher, age four today, and Ellen Gallagher, age two-and-a-half.

"Is everybody still there?" Joannie asked as he came back into the bedroom.

"All but two," he said. He flipped the snap lock on the bedroom door and started taking off his robe. "They're sound asleep," he said.

"Why did you lock the door?" Joannie asked.

"So you won't fall out of bed." He threw his robe over the back of the chair, kicked off his slippers and slid under the blankets.

"I hope you didn't misunderstand," Joannie said.

"About what?"

"About my asking you to come back to bed."

"I didn't misunderstand," he said.

"I hope not," Joannie said.

"I hope you don't misunderstand about my locking the door."

"I don't misunderstand," she said.

"I hope not."

Joannie slid over in the bed and put her head on his shoulder. "Isn't it lovely and wonderful?"

"Yes," he said, "it is."

"Isn't it wonderful that two restless people like us. . . ."

"Intermarried and mismatched . . . ," he said.

"Intermarried," she said, "and never the twain shall meet. . . ."

"It's lovely," Jim said.

"Isn't it lovely," she said, "that two restless light sleepers like us should have two lovely children who sleep so well?"

"It's very lovely," he said, "and you're a funny lady."

"That's true," she said, "I am a funny, short lady."

"And you're very sleepy," he said.

"I'm not so sleepy," she said. "Besides how can I sleep when he keeps bouncing that ball."

"You deceived me," he said. "You weren't sleepy at all."

"Count your blessings, Daddy."

▪ 2 ▪

BRIAN RAMSEY GOT UP FROM HIS BED AND WALKED INTO THE kitchen. He moved easily, with grace and balance. Like a fine-honed athlete. He was a little over medium height, thick-shouldered and narrow-hipped. His arms swung loosely at his sides as he walked easily into the kitchen. He took a bottle of water out of the refrigerator and poured himself a glass. He drank the water, rinsed out the glass, placed it bottom-up in a dish drainer, then walked back into his bedroom.

As he lay back down on the bed, his telephone rang. He lay there listening carefully. It rang five times and then stopped. He looked at his watch. After thirty seconds, the phone rang again. Three times. Then it stopped. Ramsey counted off twenty seconds, then picked up the phone and began to dial.

Several blocks away, at the corner of Turmstrasse and Franklinstrasse, a young man wearing white coveralls and a black leather cap sat behind the wheel of a pale green Volkswagen truck. Painted on the side of the truck was a Holstein cow. Beside her the pictures of a milk carton and a round carton of cottage cheese.

At the curb, no more than six feet from where the driver sat in his milk truck, was a glass-enclosed telephone booth. As the driver struck a match to relight his pipe, the phone began to ring. Five times. Then it stopped. The driver looked at his watch and waited. The phone rang again. Three times. The driver knocked out his pipe against the truck door, started the engine, and pulled out from the curb.

Ramsey stood at the wide windows of his living room, hands in pockets, looking down at the street through the half-open venetian blinds. He had turned the radio on in the kitchen and as he waited the music swirled out softly through the apartment behind him.

Slowly now, moving easily, the green truck pulled up in front of the apartment building and parked at the curb opposite the front entrance. The driver, fiddling with his pipe, looked up from behind the wheel at Ramsey's window. The blinds closed sharply, opened wide, and quickly closed again. The driver reached back into his truck, picked out a carton of milk, crossed the street and walked into the front entrance of the building. As Ramsey watched from behind the blinds, he recrossed the street, got into his truck and drove away.

Ramsey moved quickly then. Out of his apartment, past the elevator and down the service stairs. There, on the bottom step, he found a quart of milk, a picture of the black Holstein printed on the side. He picked it up and ran back up the stairs to his apartment.

Inside again, he double-locked the front door and walked quickly to the kitchen where he poured the milk out into the sink. Taking a razor blade out of a utility drawer he neatly scored the milk carton at the seams, and flattened it out into one large piece of cardboard. Wiping away the remaining milk droplets, he then began to scrape away the paraffin inside coating with the edge of the razor blade. The corner of the blade hit an obstruction and catching the edge between his thumb and forefinger, he slowly peeled away a folded square of paper. Taking it into the bathroom, he unfolded it under the strong light over the sink. On the paper, in small type, was printed one word—"Yes."

Gallagher lay on his back in the bed, his head propped on two pillows, Joannie's head on his shoulder.

"Can you see the clock?" he asked.

"No, can't you?"

"Not with your head on my shoulder, I can't."

"I can't either," she said.

"Well, make an effort, dummy."

She raised her head slightly and twisted it around so she could see the clock on the bed table behind Jim's head. Then she settled back.

"Well?" he said.

"I don't want to tell you."

"Tell me."

"It's almost seven," she said.

"I have to get up."

"I know," she said. "That's why I didn't want to tell you." As he got out of bed and started putting on his robe, she laughed softly.

"What's so funny?"

"I have a question," she said. "When did our friend stop bouncing that crazy ball?"

Wager came out of his kitchen carrying a cup of coffee. Blocky and thick-necked, he looked as though no week of his life had passed without leaving its mark on him. His right arm had been broken twice at the elbow and was two inches shorter than the left, the forefinger on his left hand was gone, and his eyes seemed to hide a pattern of scars too intricate to catalog. As he put his cup down on the desk his phone rang.

"Hello. Yes. Is this the Mobile operator? Hello? Yes, I see. Yes. What time is it there? Midnight? I thought it was only eleven. All right, operator. Yes, keep trying. Thank you."

He hung up the phone and sat down at his desk again. He took a sheet of paper out of the typewriter, folded it, put it into an envelope, addressed it and stamped it. Then he sat back in the chair with his hands folded in his lap, staring at the framed photograph of the woman and the two boys.

■ 3 ■

Ramsey, bareheaded and wearing a trim tweed suit, strolled west on Kaiserin-Augusta and turned into a little wooded park. It was early for the park. No one there. Even the children who used it as a combination playground and short cut on the way to school were not there yet. Ramsey strolled and hummed and tapped a newspaper against his leg. He looked like an ex-champion cricket player or a cross-country runner perhaps who was now on holiday from a session of advanced study at an English university.

As he meandered along, he stopped suddenly by a large tree ten or fifteen feet off the main path. He lighted a cigarette and studied the tree trunk carefully. Then, flicking the match away, he glanced about him quickly and, with one swift motion, pulled out a red thumbtack that was stuck in the bark of the tree. He dropped it into his jacket pocket and walked slowly away, slapping the folded newspaper against his leg.

Jake Gallagher opened his eyes, rolled over on his side, and scanned the nursery. Then he squirmed out of the tucked-in blankets, rolled over again and got his feet on the floor. He paused for a quick look at his sister's crib, then toddled out, droopy drawers, into the hall. He closed the door carefully behind him, mastered the stairs, the living room and the dining room, and found his father having coffee in the kitchen.

"Hello for this morning."

"Hello for this morning yourself," Jim said.

"Where's Mommy?" Jake asked.

"She's asleep."

"I want to see her," Jake said and he started out of the kitchen again.

"Wait a minute. Come back here," Jim said. Jake stopped and turned around but still seemed undecided. "Come on," Jim said. "Come on over and sit down. You can have breakfast with your daddy." With a last look at the stairs, Jake walked over and struggled up onto a chair facing Jim.

"Why can't I go see Mommy?" Jake asked.

"I think we should let her sleep."

"I'm awake," Jake said.

"I know you're awake but Mommy's asleep. You hungry?" No answer. "I said, are you hungry?"

"Why is Mommy sleeping?" Jake asked.

"Because it's early. You're up early."

"I woke up because I was hungry."

"Now we're getting somewhere," Jim said. "You want some cereal?"

"How about bananas?" Jake said.

Jim walked to the refrigerator and looked inside. "No bananas today. How about cereal?"

"How about eggs?" Jake said. "I like eggs."

"How about cereal?" Jim said, pouring some out in a bowl.

"That's my sister's cereal," Jake said.

"She won't mind," Jim said.

"Hmm?" Jake said.

Jim sat down to his coffee again and said, "I say your sister won't mind if you eat her cereal."

"Why do girls sleep so much?" Jake asked.

"Because they're poor old tired things."

"I couldn't be a girl," Jake said. "I wake up too much."

"Uh-huh," Jim said. "Eat your cereal."

On a narrow street near the Charlottenburg Palace, Ramsey walked into a tobacco shop. It was empty except for a husky, gray-haired woman who stood behind the counter.

"Do you have American cigarettes?" Ramsey asked.

"*Nein.*"

"English?" Ramsey said then.

"Only Goldflakes."

"One Goldflake, *bitte!*" As he spoke, he tapped a box of matches lightly on the counter top. When the woman's eyes

17

went at last to the box, he flipped it over. The red thumbtack was stuck in the lid. The woman stared at the matchbox, then at Ramsey, for a long moment. Then she turned her back to him and with her thick fingers selected a box of Goldflakes. The fifth box from the top. She slipped it out of the stack and placed it on the counter. Ramsey picked up the box, dropped it into his jacket pocket and walked out of the shop.

■ 4 ■

"HELLO. YES, THIS IS MR. WAGER. YES . . . I SEE. No, I guess not. You'd better cancel the call, operator. No, thanks. I'll place it later in the day."

He hung up the phone then and walked into the kitchen with his coffee cup. He looked out the kitchen window at the paved court down below. Three children with school bags over their shoulders were kicking a soccer ball back and forth.

Wager turned from the window and walked into the bedroom. He opened the closet door, took out his suit jacket and put it on. Then slowly he sank down to the edge of the bed and sat there with his head in his hands.

Gallagher stood in the center of his kitchen, fully dressed now, finishing his second cup of coffee. Jake, still at the table, his cereal bowl emptied, was drinking a tall glass of milk.

"That's a good boy," Jim said.

"I like milk," Jake said, setting his glass down.

"That's good. Now wipe off your mouth," Jim said. He handed him a paper napkin. "Did you have enough to eat?"

"How about a banana?" Jake said.

"No bananas. We don't have any bananas."

"I like bananas," Jake said.

"Sure, you do," Jim said. "Come on hot-shot, let's go see if your sister's still asleep."

"Can I wake her up with a whistle?" Jake said, sliding down from his chair.

18

"I don't think that's such a good idea," Jim said. He took Jake by the hand and they climbed the stairs to the nursery. Jim picked him up then and they both looked down into Ellen's crib. She was asleep. Jim walked over to the windows in the corner by Jake's bed and said in a whisper, "We don't want to wake your sister, do we?"

"I have a whistle," Jake said.

"I know," Jim said, "but here's what let's do instead. Daddy has to go to work now. So why don't you play in here by yourself? With your cars or something. And I'll put Ellen into bed with Mommy."

"Won't I be lonesome?" Jake said.

"I don't think so," Jim said. "Your mommy will be awake before too long." He set Jake down then, lifted Ellen carefully out of her crib and carried her down the hall to the other bedroom with Jake trailing along behind. After he tucked Ellen, still sleeping, in beside her mother, Jim picked up Jake again, went out and closed the door softly behind him.

Back in his own room, Jake said, "Won't I be lonesome?"

"A little bit maybe. But that won't hurt you."

"I'll play here with my cars," Jake said.

"That's right."

"Why did you put my sister in bed with Mommy?"

"Because your mommy doesn't like to sleep by herself."

■ 5 ■

IN THE SECTION CALLED TEGEL IN NORTHWEST BERLIN, JUST east of the lake called Tegeler See, there is an assembly plant owned and operated by the Porsche automobile combine. Fronting on Holzhauser Strasse it goes back north and west for several hundred yards in each direction. Over five thousand men work here in three eight-hour shifts per day. This is the main export facility for Porsche. From here, hundreds of cars each month are shipped to Western Europe, trained to Hamburg for shipment to Great Britain, Canada, and the

United States, and hauled by carrier to the East Zone where an exchange trade ratio has been worked out with a prewar Porsche plant which now manufactures a Russian-designed automobile.

It was five minutes to eight when Burt Wager's car pulled into the south parking lot of the plant in Tegel. As he got out of his car, Gallagher, who had pulled in just behind him, fell in beside him for the fifty-yard walk to the central traffic building. As they walked, a taxi pulled in through the main gate and Ramsey got out. As he paid the driver, Gallagher and Wager stopped to wait for him.

"Do you see what I see?" Jim said.

"Casanova in a taxicab," Wager said.

"You know what that means."

"It means," Wager said, "that he didn't make it home last night."

Ramsey walked up to them now and the three of them started toward the traffic building again.

"This *is* Friday, isn't it?" Ramsey said.

"Is this Friday, Burt?" Jim said.

"Feels like Monday to me," Wager said.

"Me, too," Jim said. "I think you're a little mixed-up, Brian. Burt thinks it's Monday and I have a strong feeling he's right."

"I have a strong feeling," Ramsey said, "that you're both a bit loose upstairs."

"Brian, did you ever think," Wager said, "that it gives the plant a bad name when you come to work in a taxi two or three mornings a week?"

"Did you ever think," Jim said, "that it gives the car itself a bad name when you don't drive it? When you're seen everywhere in a taxicab?"

"Did you two ever think that I haven't had my coffee yet?" Brian asked.

"'E 'asn't 'ad 'is cawfee yet!" Jim said.

"Whawt a pitty!" Wager said.

"If you two comedians will come to London with me," Ramsey said as they entered the glass and aluminum building, "I will personally guarantee that you will get your chance on telly."

They walked a few steps down a broad corridor and got into an elevator.

"Let's get back to your car," Jim said. "Is it really in bad shape?"

"We can't have a young export executive driving a junker," Wager said.

Jim said he would think that Ramsey would be entitled to the free use of a company car.

"I should think so," Wager said. "I would think we could jolly well get him a company car."

"Funny," Ramsey said, "you *are* a couple of droll and amusing fellows. You really must go to work on telly."

"But what about your car?" Jim said.

"It's your destiny to entertain the world," Ramsey said. "Your ruddy and undeniable destiny."

"The car," Wager said.

Ramsey said he hated to disappoint them but his car was in excellent condition. They came out of the elevator then and started down a long corridor with offices on each side. And open areas where typists and business machine operators were already at work.

"As a matter of fact," Ramsey said, "I loaned my car to a lovely Austrian girl named Anna who sings in a cabaret on Uhlandstrasse."

"A girl?" Jim said. "By Jove," he said to Wager, "he's loaned his car to a girl."

"Astounding, isn't it?" Ramsey said.

"Just shows how wrong a person can be," Wager said.

"Think of it," Jim said, "Brian Ramsey mixed up with a girl."

"It had to happen sooner or later," Ramsey said.

They turned left at the end of the corridor, walked through a reception area where several secretaries were at work and into an office with Herr Wager painted neatly on the door. On either side of his office were doors with Gallagher's and Ramsey's names on them.

Inside Wager's office, his secretary, a full-bosomed German girl with a soft voice and lovely slender legs, was pouring coffee into three cups.

"I saw you drive into the parking lot," she said in German.

"Very good, Berta. Thank you," Wager said. He walked behind his desk and sat down as the girl left the room and closed the door. "Help yourselves to coffee and pull up a chair."

Gallagher and Ramsey sat down in front of Wager's desk and the three of them drank their coffee in silence. When Wager spoke again, his tone was different. Not like the bantering in the parking lot or in the elevator or in the corridor. Friendly still. But business.

"You saw the two carriers downstairs," he said. "They're loaded and ready to go. The pickup's set for nine-thirty so you'd better get started. You go with the cars, Jim. Brian will make the pickup."

"Purple Seven. Right?" Ramsey said.

"That's right. Park on the south side and walk north. Hector will meet you in the center of the field."

"Who's driving my carrier?" Ramsey said.

"Mittag." Wager buzzed his secretary then and asked if Mittag was waiting outside. "Good," he said, "send him in." When he hung up he said to Gallagher and Ramsey, "So that's it. Routine."

Mittag came in then, a sturdy German in his early thirties. Wager spoke to him in German. "Is everything ready?" he asked.

"Yes, sir," Mittag said.

"All the contacts are made?"

"All waiting," Mittag said.

"Good," Wager said. "You'd better get going."

■ 6 ■

FIVE MINUTES LATER THE TWO CARRIERS, EACH CARRYING EIGHT gleaming new Porsches, pulled out through the front gate. Ramsey and Mittag were in the front seat of the second, Gallagher and his driver in the front seat of the first. They turned left into Holzhauser Strasse. Then bearing due east, they headed for the Wollankstrasse gate to the East Zone.

It was a routine inspection at the gate. The carriers always crossed at the same point. Gallagher's and Ramsey's faces were familiar to the guards at either end and they in turn knew most of the guards by name. Periodically, there were minute inspections of every single automobile on the carrier. And there had been occasions where upholstering had been completely removed and motors dismantled. But the cars had always been

22

clean. Consequently, the crossing was normally smooth and swift as it was this morning.

Past the gate, the carriers turned up Breite Strasse and headed northeast. As they turned due north three kilometers further on and sped up Pasewalker Strasse, Ramsey, who had been carefully watching the rearview mirror, saw a black Mercedes pull out from the curb and follow them. Gallagher, also intent on the rearview mirror, saw it too. He glanced ahead then and saw an intersection light blinking about half a kilometer away. As the carriers began to slow down for the stop, he saw that the Mercedes had pulled even with the cab of Ramsey's carrier and was slowing down now at the same rate of speed.

In the geometric swarm of cars stopped at the intersection, Gallagher saw Ramsey climb quickly down from the carrier and get into the back seat of the Mercedes. When the light changed and the carriers went straight ahead toward Buchholz, the black car turned right and headed east through the Blankenburg section.

Inside the car, Ramsey took off his blue shop coat with *Porsche* embroidered on the pocket, folded it into a neat square, and slipped it into a brown paper envelope on the seat beside him. Then he took a snub-nosed revolver out of a shoe box on the car floor, checked the loaded cylinder, and locked a silencer into place on the barrel before slipping it into his inside jacket pocket.

Suddenly the driver pulled the car over to the curb and stopped. He got out without saying a word and walked briskly up the street. Ramsey got out of the back seat, slid under the wheel and drove ahead by himself. Further north, into the Karow section of East Berlin.

Twenty minutes later, Ramsey pulled up at the edge of an empty, weedy field of rubble far up in the northeast tip of the East Zone. There are no houses, no traffic, no people here. As he sat behind the wheel and looked around, he saw only a few trees and the skeletons of half-a-dozen long-since bombed-out buildings. On the far side of the field, over a quarter of a mile away, he could see a road that came down a long hill and ran along the side of the field opposite him. He studied the road carefully. There was no one there. Not yet.

Ramsey slouched down comfortably, his head resting against the back of the seat. He took the box of Goldflakes out of his pocket, opened it all the way across the top, and turned it upside down. Although the pack was filled, only one cigarette slipped out, falling lightly into the palm of his hand. He held it in his fingers, examining it carefully. Then he put it back into the box with the other cigarettes and put the box into his pocket. He glanced at his watch now and looked back across the field. Still no one there. But, as he watched, the small silhouette of a man on a bicycle came over the hill edge and coasted slowly down the slope toward the far side of the field.

Hector slowed his bicycle down, stepped off it, and walked it along the road at the edge of the field, looking across as he moved along. When he saw a man get out of a car and start walking toward him through the knee-high weeds and grass he turned into the field himself and began walking slowly toward the center, pushing his bicycle ahead of him.

The two men met in the center of the field. From a distance they were two tiny figures. The wind had come up and was blowing the grass and blowing their clothes and making the clouds move quickly in the sky behind them. Their heads nodded as they stood in the center of the field in the wind and talked.

Hector pulled his soft felt hat down farther on his forehead. It was a strong face. The eyes were strong. And the set of the mouth. But the deep furrows in the cheeks were from laughing. And the lines at the corner of his eyes. He reached into his pocket now and took out a pack of Goldflakes. He opened it and held it out to Ramsey. There was one cigarette in the box. Ramsey fished it out, held it carefully in his fingers, then eased it into the side pocket of his jacket.

Hector turned his bicycle around now to head back across the field to the road. He was turning his head back to say good-by just as Ramsey brought the revolver up from his belt. Hector stood looking at him with a baffled expression on his face. The bullet slamming into his chest didn't change that expression. It was still there after two more shots when he lay in the tall grass tangled between the wheels of his bicycle.

On the way back across the field to the car, Ramsey found a large flat stone in the grass. He lifted it up, used the gun barrel to dig out a hollow in the damp earth, then left the revolver there in that shallow grave under the rock.

Sitting on the front seat of the car with the door open and his feet on the ground, Ramsey took the cigarette Hector had given him out of his side pocket. Carefully tearing the paper along the side he dumped the loose tobacco into his left hand. Rolling the

24

cigarette paper into a tight ball between his thumb and forefinger, he put it into his mouth and swallowed it. Then he opened his left hand flat and carefully blew all the shreds of tobacco away into the wind. Still in the palm of his hand was a tiny cylinder of microfilm no larger than a grain of buckshot. He pushed it slowly about in the palm of his hand with his right forefinger. Then he flipped it away into the tall weeds.

Twenty-five minutes later, Ramsey stopped the Mercedes in front of a fish market in the south part of Blankenburg. As he climbed into the back seat, took his blue coat out of the envelope and started to put it on, a man in a dark-blue striped suit, a fat man with gray hair, came out of the fish market, got behind the wheel and drove off. Heading west.

Fifteen minutes after that, as the two empty carriers stopped at an intersection two miles east of the wall, Gallagher looked into his rearview mirror and saw Ramsey step out of the black car and climb up into the cab of the second carrier.

As the light changed, the black car pulled ahead of both carriers, made a left turn, and headed east. Gallagher looked over at his driver and said, "All right. Let's go."

▪ 7 ▪

IT WAS A FEW MINUTES AFTER ELEVEN BY THE TIME THEY GOT back inside Wager's office. Wager came in from his secretary's desk, closed the door behind him, and sat down behind his own desk.

"How'd it go?" he said.

"Routine for me," Gallagher said. "Mittag turned all the transfer papers over to traffic central."

"No problem at the gate?" Wager asked.

"Not even a sneeze."

"How about the pickup?" Wager to Ramsey.

"Tranquil and beautiful," said Ramsey. "Hector sends his love."

"Is that all he sent?" Wager asked.

"No. He's given up smoking so he asked me to give you his last pack of Goldflakes."

"High time he gave it up," Wager said, taking the pack from Ramsey. He opened the cigarette box and turned it upside down. One cigarette fell out. He saw the box was full and he shook it but no more cigarettes came out. He looked inquiringly at Ramsey.

Ramsey nodded his head and said, "That's it."

Wager took an envelope from his desk drawer, dropped the cigarette into it, and sealed it. Then he picked up the intercom and buzzed his secretary. "Tell Mittag to get car six and wait for me downstairs. I'll be there in five minutes."

"He said it was a question of giving up his bicycle or giving up cigarettes," Ramsey said. "So he's giving up cigarettes."

Wager got up from his desk, put the envelope in his pocket, and went to his closet for a light raincoat. As he put it on he said, "That's the wisdom of maturity. He's seventy years old so now he's going to start taking care of himself."

"Next he'll be giving up women," Gallagher said.

"Never," Ramsey said.

Gallagher said that left him with nothing but the bicycle to give up.

"He won't give that up either," Wager said. "The schnapps he gave up last winter. The smoking today. But never the women and never the bicycle."

"That's right," Ramsey said. "He rides the bicycle to keep in shape so he won't have to give up the women."

"And you come to work in taxicabs," Gallagher said.

"That's something else again," Ramsey said.

Wager finished putting on his coat and came back to sit on the corner of his desk. "I may not be back today," he said. "If anything boils over, I'll be at Blue-point. Brian, you go through the motions with Friedrich in traffic. You sit here in my chair, Jim, and keep an eye on things. If I don't get back here, I'll see you tonight."

"What's tonight?" Ramsey asked.

"Jim's house," Wagner said.

"Jake's birthday," Gallagher said. "I invited you a week ago."

"Ten to one he can't make it," Wager said, "because he has to pick up his car."

"As a matter of fact," Ramsey said, "I do have to pick up my car. Sorry, Jimbo, I forgot all about it."

"He's my godson," Wager said, "and you'd better be there. Car or no car."

"Joannie will murder you if you don't show up," Gallagher said.

"Oh, I'll be there all right, but I may have to leave early," Ramsey said. "Will I be forgiven for that?"

"I guess so," Gallagher said.

"And I may be late getting there," Wager said as he walked to the door. "Will I be forgiven for that?"

Gallagher said they were both forgiven in advance. "Just show up," he said.

"We'll be there," Wager said as the three of them walked out into the reception area and stopped in front of Wager's secretary. Wager told her he was going to the Hilton for lunch but he didn't want to be disturbed there. "Jim will take all my calls. I'll be in touch with you later in the afternoon."

Ramsey leaned over the desk then, took the secretary's hand and kissed it elaborately. "If you come with me to London, I will put you in motion pictures. You will be a bigger star than Lassie."

"Come on, Dracula, she needs her blood," Wager said. "See you tonight, Jim."

"Anytime after six-thirty," Jim said.

"I'll be early," Ramsey called back as he and Wager started down the corridor.

Wager's secretary smiled at Gallagher as he went back inside the office and closed the door. She kept watching the door for a long moment after it closed. Then she got up and walked over to look down the corridor. Coming back to her desk she sat motionless, eyes fixed on Wager's office door again. Then, from the hand that Ramsey had kissed, she dropped a small folded piece of paper on her desk top. Unfolding it quickly, she read the message scrawled on it in pencil. It said: WAGER—BLUE-POINT. She flicked her cigarette lighter then and quickly burned the scrap of paper, dropping the brittle black ash in a large glass ashtray on her desk. Then, her eyes still on Wager's door, she picked up her telephone and began to dial.

◼ 8 ◼

JOAN GALLAGHER STOOD IN HER KITCHEN FINISHING THE
dinner dishes. Over her black party dress she wore a pale blue
apron. She dried her hands and looked at the clock over the
stove. Nine twenty-five. In the living room she could hear
Ramsey singing *Greensleeves*. Quietly like a lullaby. She hung
the towel over the sink, took off her apron and hung it on a hook
beside the refrigerator. Then she brushed her hair back with
one hand and went through the dining room into the living
room.

Ellen, who had been awake but drowsy ten minutes earlier,
was now asleep in her father's lap. Jake, stationed close to the
music, was in Brian's lap, fighting sleep. As his mother came
into the room he mounted his final rear-guard action and, losing
it, slipped off to sleep. Joannie sat down on the arm of Jim's
chair as they listened to Brian, in a husky, untrained voice, sing
on to the end of a stanza.

"That's all for Jake," Ramsey said then.

"He fought to the finish," Gallagher said.

Joannie took Ellen out of Jim's arms and said, "Not this poor
little thing."

"She barely got through the dessert," Jim said.

"That's all right," Joannie said, "I barely got through the
martinis."

"When your son reaches four years of age," Gallagher said,
"you mustn't count the cost."

"Or the calories," Ramsey said.

28

"Or the hang-overs," Joannie said.

"Right," Jim said. "Now—what do we do with these dead Indians?"

"I was trying to keep them awake so they could see Burt," Joannie said.

"I thought he'd be here before now," Jim said.

"I'm afraid his dinner won't be much good," Joannie said. "Even warmed up."

"Well, it won't be the first meal he's missed. In Korea I don't think he averaged one meal a day. Did he, Jimbo?"

"The South Koreans said he lived on blood," Gallagher said, "like a tiger."

"He's the sweetest tiger I've ever seen," Joannie said.

"Somehow," Ramsey laughed, "I've never thought of Burt as sweet. How about you, Jim?"

"No. I'm afraid that's not the word," Jim said.

"You're just men," Joannie said. "What do *you* know?"

"I know we've got a couple of passed-out kids here," Jim said to Joannie. "Let's put them to bed. I'll bring Jake."

"Sit still," Ramsey said. "I'll carry him up."

"That's a good idea," Joannie said. "Brian sang him to sleep. Now he can do some of the hard work."

"I will carry him upstairs," Brian said, "put him in pajamas, and put talcum on his bottom."

"He's four years old, for Pete's sake. He doesn't get his bottom talcumed any more." Jim turned to Joannie then. "Or does he?"

"Not unless he sneaks into the bathroom and does it himself," Joannie said. "Let's go, Brian." She stood up, hefted Ellen higher in her arms and started for the stairs. Ramsey picked up Jake and followed behind her.

When they were halfway up the stairs, the telephone in the downstairs hall rang. "I'll get it," Jim said.

"That's Burt, I'll bet," Joannie said.

"Give him hell for being late," Brian said.

"I will," Gallagher said, picking up the receiver.

"*Bitte*," he said as Joan and Brian disappeared into the children's room.

"Hello, Jimbo. It's Burt."

"You're late."

"I know it," Wager said. "I couldn't help it."

"The kids gave up but we haven't," Jim said. "Brian's still here and we saved some food for you."

"I already ate," Wager said. "I figured I'd missed dinner at your house so I had something down here."

"You can fight that out with Joannie," Jim said. "Come on over."

"I'll be there in twenty minutes. Tell Brian to be sure to wait for me."

"Will do," Jim said. "See you later." Gallagher hung up the phone and walked back to the living room. As he sat down, Ramsey came back downstairs and asked if it was Wager who had called.

"Yeah," Jim said. "He'll be over in about twenty minutes."

Ramsey looked at his watch and said he was due to leave. "I'm afraid I'm going to miss him."

"He said he wanted you to stick around," Jim said.

"What's up?" Ramsey said.

"He didn't say. But you know Burt," Jim said. "He only talks head-to-head."

Ramsey stood in the limbo of the hall doorway for a moment. Then he said, "Let me use your phone, will you? I'll see if I can change my appointment. Make it later."

"Help yourself," Jim said as Ramsey stepped to the hall phone and began to dial.

A few seconds later, the telephone rang in an overdecorated, thickly carpeted apartment overlooking the Kerenzberg Gardens. Cöswig's hand as he softly lifted the receiver was pale, fat and hairless. A jade ring on the forefinger. His face as the heavy-lipped mouth spoke into the phone was old and veined and evil. In deadly, fat repose.

"Yes," he said.

"I have a little complication, here," Ramsey said, "and I thought perhaps I'd come along later. How does that sound to you?"

"Come now," Cöswig said. "Come at once." He hung up the phone sharply.

Ramsey glanced back to where Gallagher was sitting in the living room. Then he went on talking into the telephone. Louder now.

"Yes, I know, honey. I know I said that. I see. Oh, that is difficult then, isn't it! All right, what shall we do? How about this? I'll come over there for a few minutes now so I can meet the fellow who's bringing the car. That's right. Then I'll come back here. Yes, I do have to come back here, darling. Then, after your second show—I'll pick you up and we'll go someplace for supper. Very good. I'll be along in a few minutes then. Good-by, Anna." He hung up the receiver and walked into Gallagher. "Well, you heard me. I tried."

"It's your business, buddy," Jim said. "But I think you should stick around."

"It'll be all right," Ramsey said. "I'll find a cab and I'll be there and back before you know it. Shouldn't be more than twenty minutes or half an hour. I'll explain to Burt when I get here. See you later, Joannie," he called up the stairs as he walked through the hall and out the front door.

▪ 9 ▪

JIM LOOKED AT THE BIRTHDAY PARTY SHAMBLES IN THE LIVING room.

Balloons, gift wrappings, toys and party favors were scattered all around. Also brandy glasses and coffee cups. He picked up the cups and saucers now and carried them out to the kitchen. As he was carefully setting them in the sink, Joannie came into the kitchen.

"That was quick," Jim said.

"I'm a quick girl," Joannie said, putting on her apron again.

"You're a degenerate," Jim said.

"That's true. Where's Brian?"

"He left but he's coming back."

"How about Burt?" she asked.

"That was him on the phone. He'll be here shortly."

"Some party," she said. "By installments."

"Burt ate already. When he saw he'd be so late he went ahead and had some dinner."

"I repeat," Joannie said. "Some party. One guest leaves early and the other comes late. Oh, well, we'll give Burt some coffee and cognac. And there's plenty of birthday cake if he wants it." They both went back into the living room and began gathering up the party debris.

"Burt sounded funny on the phone. There seems to be something he wants to talk to Brian and me about."

"Oh-oh, that means Mama-san will be sent to her bedroom to crochet place mats." Then, "Nothing serious, I hope."

"No, I don't think so. Probably won't take more than fifteen minutes. A half-hour at the most."

"Don't worry about it. I'll come down whenever you're finished." They both went to the kitchen now with handfuls of crepe paper, gift wrappings, and crushed party horns.

"It becomes increasingly apparent to me," Jim said, "that you should have married a more reliable man."

"That's true," Joannie said.

"A radish farmer, perhaps, from the Salinas Valley."

"One of my own people," she said.

"Or a greengrocer in San Luis Obispo."

"A reliable man," Joannie said, "with dependable hours and a predictable future."

"It's true," Gallagher said as they turned off the kitchen light and went back into the living room.

"Very true," Joannie said, settling down on the couch with her feet tucked under her. "Every night in my sleep, a ballet of greengrocers dances before my eyes."

Outside a car screeched to a stop. "If that's Mr. Wager," Joannie said, "he shouldn't drive so fast."

Gallagher went to the window and looked out.

"You're right. He shouldn't. But this time it's not Burt. It's the father of the shortstop next door."

"God bless that energetic child," Joannie said.

Jim came back from the window to the bar. "You want a drink?"

"I don't think so."

"Come on," Jim said, "let's have a cognac."

"Cognac makes my heart thump."

"So—let it thump." He began to pour into two small brandy glasses.

"It's true," Joannie said as she watched him. "I should have married a steady and reliable young man who wears button-down collars and seersucker suits in the summer. We would have lived in the suburbs of San Francisco and had several children and he would have commuted by bus to the city. Security and shady streets and no surprises."

Gallagher handed her a glass and sat down in the big chair facing her. "And look what you got instead," he said.

"I'm really not an adventurous soul," she said. "You know that. I could live in one neighborhood all my life and not be discontent. Adventure and . . . I don't know what . . . glamour, I suppose you'd call it, those things aren't important to me. I never thought about things like that when I imagined what my life would be like."

"And look what you got," Jim said.

"But that's the funny part," she said. "I love what I got. It's just that I thought my life would be. . . ." She sipped from her glass and looked at it in the light. ". . . Well, I guess I thought it would be cognac out of a cognac bottle. But instead it turns out to be cognac out of a . . . well, out of a champagne bottle."

"Or a beer bottle?" Jim said.

"Something like that," she said.

"But it is cognac," he said.

"No doubt about it."

"And it does make your heart thump?"

She smiled and said, "Yes, Papa." Just then another car screeched its brakes outside. "Why does Burt drive the way he does?" she said.

"He does everything that way," Jim said. "Drives fast, chain-smokes, never sleeps and drinks too much."

"That's what I mean," Joannie said. "Why is he like that?"

"Who knows," Jim said. "Brian's theory is that Burt has a compulsion to finish things."

"What does that mean?"

"I don't know," Jim said. "You'll have to ask Brian. It's just that Burt's been living a double life all these years. Twenty years as an army man and now the last six or seven here in Berlin. He's been slugging it out all this time in one lousy assignment or war or outpost after another and every day he's been wanting to throw it over and go back to Alabama where he could be with his wife and kids. The steady life."

"You mean he's like me," Joannie said.

"Maybe," Gallagher said. "At least that's what Brian thinks. Burt's a professional soldier and a family man. Two things that don't go together very well. So, he keeps driving to finish every job and every piece of every job because he's fooling himself that finally the work will be over and he can go home and start being what he wanted to be all along."

"That's sad, Jim."

"You bet it's sad," Jim said.

"How about his wife?"

"It's been rough on her, too. And on his kids. The older boy's all right, I guess. He's in college. Graduates in a year or so. But the younger one has been in some kind of trouble ever since he was twelve. Now he's seventeen and apparently he's in a real jam. Burt's secretary told Brian that the kid was arrested a couple of days ago. He ran over a woman and then left the scene of the accident. And I guess he'd been drinking. Burt's been going nuts trying to do something by phone and still keep on top of everything here."

Car brakes squealed outside then. A car turned into their driveway and the motor sound cut off.

"That's Burt," Jim said, getting up from his chair. Joannie got up too and said she would finish her cognac upstairs.

"Come and get me when your business is over."

He patted her on the bottom as she started up the stairs and said, "It won't be long."

▪ 10 ▪

WHEN GALLAGHER OPENED THE FRONT DOOR, WAGER WAS coming up the walk from his car. They walked into the living room together and Wager said, "Where's Joannie?"

"Upstairs," Jim said. "She'll be down later."

"How about Brian?"

"He'll be back in a few minutes," Jim said. "He went to pick up his car."

Wager walked further into the living room and looked around him.

"Has Joannie had any plumbers or carpenters or anybody at all working here in the house?"

"Nobody," Gallagher said. "Nobody comes unless I'm here."

"Have Swanson's men checked you out lately?"

Gallagher said they had gone over the whole house ten days ago. "And I had them come again this afternoon because I knew you and Brian would be here tonight."

34

"Were you here when they came today?"

"No, but Joannie was. And she knows Swanson's men. He always sends one of two teams. Sergeant Field and Corporal Julius. Or Sergeant Blackman and Pfc. Bohannon. Bohannon and Blackman came today."

Wager asked if they'd found anything.

"Nothing," Gallagher said. "I checked with Swanson's office myself. Late this afternoon."

"All right," Wager said. "Sit down."

Gallagher asked him if he wanted a drink.

"Hell yes, I want a drink. How soon did you say Brian would be back?"

"Half an hour or so. You want bourbon?"

"Yeah. A little water. All right, I'll fill him in when he gets here."

"We're not hot, are we?" Gallagher said.

"I hope not. But I don't like the smell of it," Wager said. "We processed the film that Brian picked up from Hector."

"And . . ." Gallagher said. He walked over to Wager and handed him his glass.

"Blue-point can't figure it out. The whole thing is a rehash of figures and photographs of installations that we had six months ago. It looks like either a switch or a plant."

"But that stuff came from Hector," Jim said. "Hand-to-hand to Brian."

"I know. And Hector doesn't shoot blanks like that."

"Did Blue-point try to contact him?" Jim asked then.

"All day. Ever since they developed the film. And that's another thing that doesn't smell right."

"Can't they find him?" Jim asked.

"Nobody's seen him since early this morning. Before he made the drop."

"What about the newsstand?" Jim asked.

Wager said it hadn't been opened up today. Jim said maybe Hector was shacked up somewhere.

"Maybe," Wager said. "But if he is, it's someplace where he's never been shacked up before. Two men on motorbikes are tracing the route all the way to Purple Seven. They should check in soon." He looked at his watch. "I wish Brian would get his ass back here."

"He should be here before long," Jim said.

Wager lighted a cigarette, took a long drink from his glass and said, "Something else happened today. It may not mean

35

anything but I've been thinking about it. When I parked my car on Wilhelmstrasse, I got out and walked a few blocks, the way I always do, to make sure there was no tail on me. Then I doubled back through that little park with the underground parking lot. You know where it is."

"Yeah, I've left my car there several times," Jim said.

"Well, when I came out of the park and started across the street, a car came through the intersection like a bat out of hell, ran a red light, and missed me by a whisker. Whoever was driving knew what he was doing. He had no plates on the back and he took the next corner on two wheels."

"I don't like the sound of that."

"Neither do I," Wager said. "If somebody's pinned a target on me, that means we've sprung a leak."

"And if your picture's up on somebody's bulletin board, then so is Brian's."

"That's right. And so is yours." Wager drained his glass and stood up. "Let me see what I can find out about Hector."

While Wager was on the phone, Jim made him another drink and filled his own cognac glass. Wager hung up and came back into the room then.

"They found Hector with three bullets in his chest," Wager said. "He never got away from Purple Seven. Looks like he's been dead since morning."

"Somebody must have tailed him and jumped him after Brian left."

"Sounds that way," Wager said. "That's the way it sounds all right." He looked at his watch. "Look, I'm going down to Center. When Brian comes back, tell him to wait here till I contact him. And I mean *wait*. I don't want to have to look for him in every pussy parlor on Uhlandstrasse."

"Why don't I go with you?" Jim said.

"I'd rather have you here where I can find you. I have a feeling in my belly that I don't like. Remember those pretty brown hills in Korea?"

"I remember all right. There was a machine gun on top of every one of them."

"Yeah, that's what I mean," Wager said, moving to the front door. "Keep your shoes on, Jim. I'll contact you later." As he started to open the door, the phone rang.

"Just a minute," Jim said. "Maybe that's Brian." He picked up the receiver. "Hello, yeah. No, Burt's right here." He held the phone out to Wager. "It's Brian."

36

"You're an elusive bastard," Wager said into the phone. "Where are you?"

Brian was sitting at a desk in Cöswig's apartment. Beside him stood Cöswig, an earphone held to his ear listening to the conversation. Behind them a black-haired man with shell-rimmed glasses waited, carefully peeling an orange.

"I'm at a *Konditorei* on Villegate," Ramsey said. "Between Barstedt and Ulmstrasse. I just stopped in here to call you. To tell you I was on my way."

"I'm just leaving here," Wager said. "So stay where you are. I'll pick you up as soon as I can get there. It should be about ten or fifteen minutes."

Ramsey glanced quickly at Cöswig, who shook his head emphatically. "Look, Burt, this place is closing up. Why don't I. . . ."

"Then wait outside," Wager said, looking at his watch. "It's eleven now. I'll be there at exactly eleven-fifteen." He hung up the phone and turned to Gallagher. "I'll pick Brian up and take him down to Center with me."

Ramsey replaced the receiver and turned to Cöswig whose face was very red as he put down the earphone. He spoke rapidly in German and waved his hand toward the door. He was still speaking when Ramsey and the man in shell rims hurried out of the apartment, and when he had closed the door and was alone Cöswig still muttered angrily to himself.

At Gallagher's front door Wager said, "If you haven't heard from me by midnight, go to bed. Until then, stay close to the phone."

"I'll be here," Jim said.

■ 11 ■

GALLAGHER LOCKED THE FRONT DOOR AS WAGER'S CAR changed gears smoothly and drove away up the quiet street. Then he went back into the living room, picked up Wager's glass and his own and carried them into the kitchen. He rinsed them under the faucet and left them on the drainboard. Then he turned off the kitchen light, turned off all the downstairs lights except for one lamp by the phone, and climbed the stairs to the children's room. Leaving their door open, he straightened their blankets in the dim light from the hall. Then he came out again, quietly closing the door behind him. In his own room the bedside lamp was full on, but Joannie, lying on her back, her head on a pillow and a book open beside her, was sound asleep. He sat down beside her and looked at her face as she slept.

"Hey," he said. No answer. "Hey," he said, shaking her gently with one hand. "I thought you were the lady who couldn't sleep alone."

"Mmmm," Joannie said, turning her face away from the light.

"Hey," Jim said after a moment. "The house is on fire." Joannie lay quietly, her face smooth and lovely. "Do you want the old man to put you to bed?" No answer.

Jim slid further down on the edge of the bed and gently lifted her skirt. He unfastened her garters and slowly, carefully peeled off her nylons. "You really *are* asleep, aren't you?" He picked her up then and carried her over to the other side of the room by her dressing table. He eased her feet down to the floor and held her standing against him. He unfastened the back of her dress and pulled it over her head. Then still holding her against him, he unfastened her brassiere and took it off. With his arm around her waist, he slipped her half-slip and underpants down to the floor. He held her then, naked and still sleeping against him. For a long moment, he stood there with his arms around her. With her head on his chest. Then he picked her up, carried her back to the bed and tucked her between the sheets. He switched off the lamp and said in a low voice, "Good night, old lady." Then in the dim light from the street, he crossed the room and let himself out into the hall.

As he pulled the door shut behind him, the phone rang downstairs. He ran down the stairs and picked it up.

"Hello."

"This is Burt, Jim. Go to bed. I won't need you tonight." Wager was standing in an outdoor telephone booth on a dark street. Wedged into the doorway, listening closely, was the black-haired man with the shell-rimmed glasses. His face was calm and his hands were in his pockets.

"What about Brian, Burt? Did you find him?"

"I'll see you tomorrow, Jim." Wager hung up and looked at the man in glasses.

Gallagher hung up the phone slowly. He picked it up then as if he were going to dial a number. But he stopped, put it back down, and started up the stairs, unbuttoning his shirt as he went. As he pulled out his shirttail and started to open his bedroom door, the phone rang again. He ran quickly down the stairs.

"Hello," he said.

"Yeah, Jimbo, I'm sorry I couldn't call sooner," Ramsey said. "Is Burt there?"

"No," Gallagher said. "He's on his way to meet you."

"What do you mean?" Ramsey asked.

"You know what I mean. When you called here and told him where to meet you, he left right away."

"What are you talking about?" Ramsey said. "I didn't call you!"

"You didn't call here and tell Burt to meet you on Villegate?"

"No," Ramsey said. "That's what I'm trying to tell you. I couldn't get to a phone till just now."

"You're nuts. I talked to you myself," Jim said.

"Jim, I'm telling you, I didn't call. I haven't called your house since I left there an hour ago."

"I don't know what's going on but we'd better find Burt. Where are you right now?"

"I'm here with Anna," Ramsey said, "on Uhlandstrasse."

"All right. Now listen to me. There's a *Konditorei* on Villegate between Barstedt and Ulmstrasse. That's where Burt's heading. I'll meet you there as fast as you can make it."

"Right," Ramsey said. Then, "Oh, Jim, wait a minute. I know that block. There's a little park on the corner. Where Barstedt runs into Villegate. Let's meet there. We can see the whole block from that corner."

"All right," Jim said. "On the corner. Get moving, buddy." He hung up the phone, grabbed a jacket out of the hall closet and, putting it on quickly, came back to the phone and dialed a number.

"Hello, Blue-point. This is Torso Two. Repeat. Torso Two. I'm calling a fire drill. Corner of Barstedt and Villegate. Come *now*. Repeat—*right now*. And alert Center for a possible bail-out. Repeat. Alert Center for a possible bail-out of the Torso Net."

Back to the closet, Jim took down a box from the top shelf,

took an automatic out of it, checked the clip, and put it into his jacket pocket. He put the box back on the shelf and closed the closet door. Then he quietly let himself out of the front door.

Upstairs in the bedroom, Joannie sat up in bed. She turned on the bed lamp and listened to the sound of a car backing out of the driveway. She slipped out of bed on Jim's side, picked up his robe off the back of the chair and wrapped it around her as she went to the window. She opened the shades just as Jim turned sharply across the curbing, shifted gears and drove off up the street. She stood there looking out at the dark houses across the way. Then she turned back, walked over to the bed and began smoothing the pillow and the sheets where she had been sleeping.

■ 12 ■

IN THE BASEMENT GARAGE OF A HIGH-RISE OFFICE BUILDING two blocks west of Spandau Citadel, a tall Negro wearing a brown business suit and a checked cap stood beside the open front door of a blue Oldsmobile. In the back seat two men wearing dark-green German raincoats sat waiting, their eyes on the door of the elevator. As they watched, the floor lights began to blink on and off as the car descended. One of the men said, "Here he comes."

The elevator door slid smoothly open then and a short man with thick red hair walked across the garage floor to the car and got into the front seat. As the Negro slid in behind the wheel and closed the door, the redhead glanced at the men in the back seat, then faced forward again and said, "Let's go." The garage door silently lifted and descended as the car rolled up the wide ramp and into the street. "Turn left on Juliusturm," the redhead said. He sat back then and lit a cigarette as the car sped east toward the center of Berlin.

Gallagher pulled his car to the curb at an intersection and looked at the street sign. Ulmstrasse. He turned left and followed the curving street northeast toward Villegate. Ten minutes later, at the corner of Ulmstrasse and Villegate he pulled his car over to the curb again and switched off the headlights. Straight ahead of him, across the street, was the *Konditorei*. Still open but not busy apparently. A few couples strolled along in the pleasant summer night. Bicycles rolled past. And a few automobiles. But no heavy traffic. No stress or commotion. An ice cream night.

Gallagher started his engine again and turned right into Villegate. Staying in the lane near the curb, he cruised slowly to the end of the block, his eyes scanning the street. At the corner of Barstedt and Villegate he pulled next to the curb, his motor idling, as cars in the center lanes passed him, moving up and down Villegate. Straight ahead of him, across Barstedt, behind the bus-stop shelter and a glass phone booth, was the park. There were no cars parked near the corner. No people waiting. No sign of Ramsey. Only a man standing in the glass phone booth, his back to the street.

Gallagher turned right around the corner, drove half a block down Barstedt and parked his car in the darkness under the trees.

As the redhead's car turned south across Richard-Wagner-Platz, he asked the Negro if they were halfway there yet.

"Almost. But it's going to be slower going now. There's more traffic now. Between here and there."

Gallagher got out of his car and walked back north along Barstedt, staying on the dark side of the street opposite the park. At the corner, he sat down on a bench in the shadows and carefully studied the scene across the way. Still no one waiting. Just occasional strollers. The bus-stop shelter with the half-lit park in the background. And the man in the phone booth. Still there talking.

Gallagher waited. Nothing. Then he slowly got up and walked to the curb. He paused there and looked back across Villegate toward the *Konditorei*. Then he crossed the street toward the park. At the bus shelter he turned, hands in pockets, and looked down the street in the direction the bus would come from. Then he turned back slowly and looked again at the phone booth. The man was still there. Deliberately Gallagher took a coin from his pocket and walked over to the phone booth. He tapped on the glass door with his coin. The man's back was to him. He didn't move. Gallagher moved around behind the booth, scanning the park entrance and the street. Then he turned to see the face of the man in the phone booth. The eyes were wide open and the mouth hung open loosely and a steady crimson rivulet oozed out of the man's sleeve and dripped from his thumb to the floor of the phone booth.

"Burt!" Gallagher said. "Jesus Christ."

He stood frozen for a long moment. Then he eased back a step or two toward his car, looking around again at the street. Nothing. He flipped the coin in the air, caught it, and put it back into his pocket. Then, softly whistling between his teeth, he turned and walked easily along the path into the park. As he disappeared among the tree shadows, a car turned off Villegate into Barstedt, its lights off. It crawled down the street and pulled into the curb a couple of car lengths ahead of Gallagher's car.

■ 13 ■

INSIDE THE PARK, GALLAGHER WALKED SLOWLY ALONG THE winding paths, his eyes exploring the half-lighted areas on either side. A boy and girl came toward him, holding hands. As he passed them they turned off and walked away from the path under the trees.

Gallagher turned back then. He walked faster now. Back toward the lights at the corner. Still in the shadows he looked out at the street, at Wager's body still wedged in the phone booth. Then he saw the car parked just ahead of his. And as he stepped out into the light he heard a husky whisper coming from that direction.

"Jimbo."

Ramsey, sitting behind the steering wheel, turned halfway in his seat to watch Gallagher walk slowly down the opposite sidewalk toward him. The man with shell-rimmed glasses, also in the front seat, locked a silencer into position on a Luger, and handed it to Ramsey.

As Gallagher reached a position on the sidewalk opposite Ramsey's car, the blue Oldsmobile pulled up in front of the *Konditorei* on Villegate.

"There's the park right up ahead," the redhead said.

Ramsey watched Gallagher. He looked in both directions and as he stepped off the curb, Ramsey brought up the gun. When he fired, he could see Gallagher's face in the light spill-over from the corner. In a crazy, stop-action kind of moment then, there flashed a look of surprise, then shock from the impact of the bullet, then blood on his face, fast glimpse, exploding down across the eyes, then the hand half-covering the face before the body stiffened and fell straight over backwards, the head and shoulders on the grass between the curb and the sidewalk, the legs stretched out into the street.

As the redhead's car turned into Barstedt, Ramsey's car screeched out from the curb and raced away down the dark street. The Negro hit the brakes and the redhead and the two men from the back seat exploded out of the car. The redhead ran quickly to Gallagher, flashed a light on his face, then stood up and fired three shots at Ramsey's car as it turned the corner a block away. Seconds later, as the redhead knelt beside Wager's body, where they'd stretched it out beside the phone booth, and as he walked then to the Oldsmobile and began talking into the phone in the front seat, Joannie Gallagher sat in the big chair in the living room. She was reading and she wasn't worried. Or so she told herself.

In a booth in a thick-carpeted restaurant on Moritzplatz, Cöswig sat talking on the telephone, a cigar between his sausage fingers, a bottle of Courvoisier at his elbow, a bowl of strawberries covered with Kirsch and thick cream in front of him. He grunted into the telephone, an overfed smile on his thick lips. Beside him sat a thin twelve-year-old girl, her hair curled and lacquered against her head, her cheeks rouged, her small mouth made larger and brighter with lipstick. Her dress was yellow, loose, and low-cut. All evening the waiters had religiously attended this table, serving, clearing, dusting crumbs, filling glasses and bending low to stare at the twelve-year-old breasts, naked inside the yellow dress. The girl stared straight ahead. Cöswig hung up the phone now, drained his brandy glass, and began spooning the strawberries and cream into his red chaos of a mouth. Still eating and without looking at the girl beside him, he lazily slid one fat

43

hand down inside the front of her dress. The girl lighted a cigarette and stared straight ahead.

▪ 14 ▪

NEAR THE SCHÖNEBERG TOWN HALL, AN AMERICAN ARMY ambulance turned out of Grunewaldstrasse and raced south-west down Hauptstrasse.

In the front seat of the blue Oldsmobile, the redhead sat at the telephone, talking urgently. On a strip of grass at the edge of the park, near where he had fallen, Gallagher lay stretched motionless on his back, the Negro and one of the raincoated men kneeling over him. At the corner three German policemen and several military policemen stood guard, block-ing off Barstedt from all cars and pedestrians.

The redhead kept telephoning. And every call set some person in motion. In apartments and furnished rooms and restaurants all over the city men and women answered, listened, hung up their phones and went into action. The Torso net was bailing out.

The army ambulance turned into Barstedt then and glided to a stop near where Gallagher lay. As the attendants prepared to load him onto the stretcher, the redhead left his car and walked quickly over to them. He talked to the doctor and to the ambulance driver. Then he talked briefly with the Negro and with each of the raincoated men before he hurried back to the Oldsmobile, got in, and drove off down Barstedt. At the first intersection he turned right and headed northwest toward Gallagher's house. Behind him, the two army doctors settled Gallagher into the ambulance and, as the motor started and they moved away from the curb, they adjusted the plasma rig over his chest.

A black car with three men inside pulled into the front gate of the Porsche plant. One man turned the car around, parked it near the gate, and began talking in German to the gate guard.

44

The other two men, each carrying a large suitcase, hurried into the administration building.

Not far away, at Flughafen Tegel, a U.S. Army transport plane stood just outside its hangar, swarmed over by coveralled mechanics and being fueled up by a hose from a red truck.

The redhead turned into the driveway beside Gallagher's house and got out of the car. Joannie got up from the chair, switched on the hall light, and was waiting with the front door open when he came up the walk from the driveway.

In Wittenau and Steglitz and Kreuzberg and Siemensstadt, all over Berlin, the people who had received calls from the redhead or from Blue-point or from other contacts down the line were on the move now. Empty-handed and without panic or haste. Deliberately. On foot or riding bicycles or streetcars or taxicabs, each of them was calmly and methodically going underground. They had done it before. And it would have to be done again. Many times perhaps. So do it. Don't attract attention. Just get lost for a while.

At the Porsche plant, the two men who had gone inside came back out to the car. The suitcases were heavy now. Inside them were all the files, employment records and personal effects of Wager, Brian Ramsey, and Jim Gallagher.

Back at the corner of Barstedt and Villegate everything was silent now. Tranquil and empty. No shattered glass, no bloodstains, no hang-over of turbulence in the atmosphere. A big, bright-lighted city bus rolled down Villegate and stopped at the corner in front of the shelter. A young man with long hair, wearing a canvas jacket, got off the bus, pulling a black-haired girl along behind him. They stopped and kissed in the full light of the streetlamp and as the bus pulled away they walked, with their arms around each other, into the park.

The redhead came out of Gallagher's house carrying Jake, still asleep, wearing pajamas and wrapped in a blanket. Behind him, Joannie, carrying Ellen, closed the door and locked it behind her. Her face was pale in the headlight's beam as she passed through it to get into the car. But there was only the paleness. She wasn't crying. The redhead turned left and headed north through the city streets toward Flughafen Tegel.

Further east, the army ambulance was also speeding through the near-empty streets toward Tegel. In the back, the doctors were bent closely over Gallagher. His face in the overhead light was gray and immobile. His breath was weak. There was no

45

flicker of eyelids. The plasma flowed and the doctors worked on as the ambulance turned right on Franklinstrasse and headed northwest toward the *Flugplatz*.

Cöswig finished his strawberries now and sipped from a freshly filled cognac glass. The girl beside him sat as rigid as before, looking straight ahead out of beaded lashes and shadowed sixty-year-old eyes.

All over the city or moving out of it in some cases, the random international leftovers who had provided the flesh if not the skeleton of the Torso net moved more slowly now. Each step or wheel-revolution away from their respective departure points, away from deadly specific addresses, gave them new confidence in their anonymity. They began, still in deliberate flight, to settle into the new identities and circumstances they had selected for themselves.

■ 15 ■

As the redhead, picked up a few blocks away by another car and escorted now, threaded his car through the outer complexes of the airport and out through the open gateway onto the concrete apron and under the belly of the waiting plane, he saw that the ambulance was just pulling in there also. The activity began.

While a tech. sergeant and an army nurse helped Joannie and the children up the stairs and into the plane, the redhead held a hurried conference with an army major and a captain. They were joined by the pilot and the four men walked forward under the wing while the redhead talked. The ambulance driver came over then and said, "The patient's aboard, sir. Major Wainright is ready whenever you are."

Inside the plane there were ten bucket seats up front but the rest of the interior was stripped. Behind the entrance, the whole tail area had been converted into an emergency hospital room. Gallagher lay on a table-height bed with straps fastened firmly across his chest and legs and a white bandage covering the upper part of his head. Two doctors, the sergeant, and an army nurse were there with Gallagher in the tail of the plane. Up front, a second army nurse was helping Joannie to settle the children, still sleeping, into seats. The redhead walked to the back of the plane. "All right, Sergeant," he said. "Close it up and let's go."

As the plane taxied down the runway, the redhead sat, seat-belted, talking with one of the doctors. As soon as they were in the air, he went up front to sit with Joannie.

Cöswig came out the front entrance of the restaurant, the girl following a few steps behind him, and stood under the canopy near the curb. The girl shivered in the night air as the doorman lighted Cöswig's cigar. As soon as the car pulled up to the curb, she hopped into the back seat like a small animal. Cöswig stood a moment longer at the curb, enjoying his cigar and surveying the night. Just before he got into the back seat, he glanced up at the sky and saw a plane, its red lights blinking, climbing away from Berlin and turning in a slow arc toward the west.

Inside the plane, one of the nurses was sitting near the children. Joannie was back in the tail of the plane now. Sitting beside Gallagher in the turned-down light. Her hands in her lap, sitting there quietly.

■ 16 ■

It was raining in London. Three o'clock in the morning and raining. The nurses wrapped army raincoats around Jake and Ellen before they carried them from the transport to a big Air Force jet standing thirty yards away. The redhead stood away from the transferal activity, coat collar turned up and hands in pockets, talking urgently to a slim middle-aged man with thinning brown hair and rimless glasses. When the tech.

sergeant came up to the two men and said, "We're all set, sir. Ready to take off," the man with rimless glasses followed him back to the jet and got on board. The redhead stood in the rain and watched the plane take off. He watched it till it climbed out of sight.

As the plane was flying over western Ireland, Jake woke up.

"Where's Mommy?" he asked the nurse, who was sorting through a package of children's clothes that had been put on the plane in London.

"She's in the back with your daddy."

"I want to go back there, too."

"No, I think you'd better stay here."

"I'm hungry."

"Well, here's a couple of cookies. Eat those and go back to sleep."

While he chewed, Jake raised up to look over the back of his seat.

"Why is my daddy lying down with that white hat on his head?"

"Your daddy had an accident. That's a bandage on his head."

"Is he sick?" Jake said.

"No. Not now. He's much better."

"Then why is Mommy sitting beside him like that?"

"She wants to be close by in case he wakes up and needs her."

"What if he wakes up and needs *me*?" Jake said.

"Then I'll wake you and tell you."

"All right. I guess I'll finish my cookies and go back to sleep."

"That's a good idea," the nurse said. "You go back to sleep."

The darkness broke up behind the plane as it flew westward and as it circled New York City and landed at last at La Guardia, the dawn came in too, grayly lighting the runways and silhouetting the hangars and waiting planes and the mechanics bustling around the jet as it taxied to a standstill in an isolated area far down the strip from the commercial terminals.

In the back seat of a black Chrysler limousine a gray-haired man, wearing a tweed topcoat with a Chesterfield collar, sat waiting. In the front seat were two neatly dressed, hatless young men, each of them with the sturdy, clean and anonymous look of a high school basketball coach.

The plane door slid open then and the gray-haired man watched intently as the sergeant, the man with rimless glasses,

48

one of the nurses, and at last Joannie and the children came down the steps and hurried into a passenger reception building a few yards away. A doctor came off the plane then, walked over and got into the car beside the gray-haired man. After a few minutes, they left the car together and climbed the steps to the plane.

Joannie came out of the building in a few minutes, leading the children, now dressed in the clothes the nurse had brought on in London, to the black limousine. As one of the clean young men helped her settle the children in the back seat, the gray-haired man came down the steps of the plane, signaled the two doctors to go back up, and called to her.

"Mrs. Gallagher." He walked to meet her as she turned away from the car. Taking her arm as he spoke, he led her a few feet away from the others, up into the shadow under the plane's wing. "I'm Harry MacNeal, Mrs. Gallagher. From Washington. The doctor tells me your husband is out of danger."

"Yes," Joannie said, "the doctor told me he'll be all right."

"He's a lucky man," MacNeal said.

"Yes. The bullet cut right across the top of his skull."

"He's a very lucky man."

"Thank God," Joannie said.

"He seems to be getting some of his strength back already."

"Yes," Joannie said. "I think he is."

MacNeal asked her then if Jim had talked to her during the flight from London. She said he had. A little.

"Did he say anything to you?" MacNeal asked her.

"How do you mean?"

"Well, he wouldn't talk to me at all. I just wanted to make sure that—well—that he's not in shock."

"What did the doctors say?"

"I didn't ask them about this. I wanted to talk with you first."

"He can talk," Joannie said, "but he hasn't said very much."

"I'm sure this has been a terrific shock to him."

"They were his two best friends," Joannie said.

"There may still be some news about Ramsey."

"I hope so," Joannie said. "I hope he's all right."

"How about your children?" MacNeal said. "Are they all right?"

"Yes," Joannie said, "they think it's all a game. They love to fly."

"Well, they're going to get a chance to fly a little further. Washington thinks that your husband and all of you should be out of sight for awhile. We're sure there's no danger now that you're away from Berlin, but we don't want to take any chances."

Joannie asked him where they were going and he said first they would drive to the Newark airport. "The doctors say your husband can sit up now so he'll ride in the car with us."

"Then where?" Joannie asked.

"Then you'll be taking another plane, a small jet, to St. Louis."

"St. Louis?"

"Yes. We have a farm about sixty miles from there that we use sometimes. It's a fine modern place and there's a nice couple there who take care of everything. Also a doctor and a nurse and two of our men from Washington will be going along with you. Your children will like it and it will be a good place for Mr. Gallagher to rest up and give his head a chance to heal."

"Couldn't we just go home to California?" Joannie asked.

"For the moment," MacNeal said, "we think this a better idea."

Joannie asked how long they would be there and MacNeal said not longer than a week or two, he hoped. "We want you in a safe place till we get some better information about what happened last night in Berlin. Then we'll go on from there."

"Then can we go home?" Joannie asked.

"Probably. We'll have to wait and see." MacNeal glanced up then and saw the sergeant and one of the doctors coming down the plane steps. Between them, leaning heavily on their shoulders, was Gallagher, the white bandage covering the top of his head like a helmet. They walked slowly to the limousine and, as the mechanics and airport workers looked on, he got into the front seat with one of the doctors and the sergeant who slid in under the wheel. MacNeal got into the back seat with Joannie and the children, and the two sturdy young men rode the jump seats. One of the mechanics, a man with a broken nose and a white scar dividing his left eyebrow, watched intently as the car backed up, turned around and drove off swiftly down the concrete apron. A hundred and fifty yards away was a wire fence. As he watched, the limousine pulled up to the fence, a gate was swung open, and the car rolled out on the expressway. As it disappeared in the inbound traffic, the mechanic wiped his hands on a soft rag, strolled inside the hangar and took a drink from the water fountain. Then he walked casually over to a pay telephone booth, settled inside it, and began to dial.

▪ 17 ▪

INSIDE THE BLACK CAR NO ONE SPOKE AS IT ROLLED SWIFTLY along toward the city. No one but the children. They were delighted by everything they passed along the way. Jake pointed out everything he saw to his sister. They laughed and shouted and asked questions as the car moved off the expressway and down Queens Boulevard to the tunnel. Bread trucks and cemeteries and ferris wheels and supermarkets, airport buses and children on bicycles. All these things delighted them as they laughed and pointed their way across mid-Manhattan to the Lincoln Tunnel and out onto the turnpike leading to the airport. There was silence in the front seat and in the back no one spoke either. Just Joannie occasionally answering a question or explaining some mystery in a low voice. And the children laughing. And the tires whirring and singing as they sped around curves on the turnpike headed for Newark.

Thirty minutes later, MacNeal stood on the second-story observation platform watching the Lear jet taxi into position far out on the runway. He watched it take off and climb and begin a lazy circle toward the southwest. Then he turned and walked back through the terminal toward the parking area.

A tall woman, wearing a three-piece gray suit and a yellow silk turban, followed leisurely behind him toward the terminal. She stopped then, tore a page from a small pad of paper and crumpled it in her hand. Then she hurried on toward the exit. Just before she went out the door, she dropped her cigarette

51

into a tall urn filled with sand. As she walked away, a man's hand reached down, pushed his own cigarette into the sand and, in the same movement, picked up the crumpled piece of paper that was half-covered there. Swinging his hand easily at his side, he crossed the reception area and walked into the men's room. Taking a dime from his pocket, he unlocked a pay toilet door, stepped inside, and closed the door behind him. Smoothing the paper out in the palm of his left hand, he held it up a little to catch the light from outside the cabinet. On the paper, printed in black letters, it said, "ST. LOUIS."

part **II**

■ 1 ■

It was a good-sized farm, nearly four hundred acres, and Gallagher, it seemed, paced and prowled every foot of it. While the children played with the nurse or with their mother in the side yard or in the orchard behind the house, while Robert Lloyd, the farmer, and his wife Mary attended to their chores at the barn, in the kitchen, in the feeding lots and chickenhouses, while Maslow and Harris, MacNeal's two men from Washington, dressed like farm hands, stayed near to the house or near to Gallagher, he walked.

From the early morning hours just after breakfast, in great looping slow circles, he walked across the black plowed earth with green corn coming up, through the grass and hollows and along the creek of the pasture land, through the clumps of yellow pine and sycamore, and the high stands of cedar. In the shade there he sat down sometimes, wild roses and hawthorn and goldenrod coloring the spaces between the trees and scenting the warm dusty air, and had a midday sandwich that he'd carried with him from the kitchen.

Every second day, in the morning early, the nurse and doctor who had come along from Berlin examined his head wound, cleaned it, and changed the bandage. The bandage got smaller as the days went by until at last it was only a two-inch square of gauze on his forehead.

It was a quiet time, an eddy at the edge of the current. Gallagher said almost nothing and the others, focusing on him and taking his rhythm as their own, also spoke very little. Mr. Lloyd, always a quiet man, and Maslow and Harris, experienced journeymen in a silent trade, spoke quietly and not often among themselves. Joannie spoke to Mrs. Lloyd and she took a minor part in mealtime conversations but she too, other than her conversations with the children, was silent and apart. The doctor and the nurse, both miserably involved in the final fluttering heartbeats of a love affair that had begun a year and a half earlier in Munich, had used up all their words long since, and even Mary Lloyd, famous county-fair cook and prize winner and irrepressible kitchen monologist, was, it seemed, strangely silent.

Like Gallagher, the others moved in an intricate pattern of overlapping circles. Slowly, leisurely and without, or so it seemed, objective or target. Only the children lived fully and noisily and in straight connecting lines. They tumbled and laughed and explored and ring-around-the-rosied with the nurse and their mother. They gobbled and spilled and pouted and cried and played hide-and-seek in the orchard. And all the while, the children in action, the adults in silence, a gray Plymouth sedan traced the perimeter of the Lloyd farm, a brown-haired woman in a cheap tan cotton coat behind the wheel, two men, one bald, the other pale as an invalid, in the back seat. Always with binoculars. Stopping at all vantage points and surveying the farm. Watching Gallagher as he walked, as he stopped under the trees, as he turned back, at the end of the day, toward the house. And a third man, permanently bivouacked in a thicket on a hill three-quarters of a mile straight west of the farm's gate, kept his binoculars tirelessly there, on the gate to the road.

At night, dinner finished and the children sleeping, the Lloyds sat together in the porch swing, talking quietly together of Fred Allen, Spencer Tracy, Alfred Landon, and organic fertilizer. Maslow and Harris played euchre on the kitchen-table oilcloth and the doctor and nurse strolled out across the orchard in an attempt to solve their intricate problems by simply being naked in the grass together.

In the bedroom, in the dark, a warm breeze blowing in across them, Jim and Joannie lay side by side in the carved oak double bed, he on his back and she on her side, facing the window. They pretended to be asleep and each knew that the other was pretending. But there was no strain between them. Just a feeling of mutual impatience for the waiting time to be over, for the eddy to stop its silent swirling and re-enter the cold rush of the stream.

▪ 2 ▪

GALLAGHER SAT AT THE KITCHEN TABLE WITH A CUP OF COFFEE
in front of him. His bandage had been taken off three days
before. Now there was a red scar, the width of a pencil, on his
forehead. It started halfway up between his left eyebrow and
his hairline and went straight up until it disappeared under
his hair. He touched it lightly with his fingertips as he sat there,
the breakfast dishes cleared away and washed and draining
now in a rack beside the sink, and everyone outside the house
except him.

Somewhere in the back of the house he could hear a radio
playing and the murmur of Joannie's voice and Mrs. Lloyd's as
they moved through the rooms making the beds. Outside he
could hear the children, operating at maximum volume and
efficiency already, and the nurse laughing and talking with
them.

Gallagher stared out the window beside the sink for a long
time, drinking coffee, refilling his cup, and drinking again. And
staring out the window, his fingertips occasionally coming back
to the scar. And hearing the radio and the voices and the
children and feeling the motion of the eddy as he sat alone and
slowly rhythmically floated in a neat circular movement inside
it.

He got up then. Abruptly. He walked to the sink, rinsed out
his coffee cup and placed it upside down on the drainboard.
Then he crossed the kitchen, went out through the screen door,
and started walking toward the barn. Straight down the half-

mile hard-packed dirt road, flanked on either side by a line of poplars, across the wooden bridge over the creek, washed-out three times in five years, Mr. Lloyd said, and up the gentle rise leading to the barn lot. Maslow and Harris were there, in their farm clothes, fixing a broken slat in the gate leading to the feeding lots. Knowing a straight line when they saw one, sensing that the long curving days were over, they came through the gate to meet Gallagher.

"Do you expect to be in touch with Washington today?" Jim said.

"Probably not," Harris said.

"Have you been in touch with them in the last couple of days?"

"Well, you see," Maslow said, "we can't. . . ."

"You don't have to play secrets with me. I don't want a floor plan of the Pentagon. I just want to know when you talked with MacNeal last."

"Don't get hard-nosed about it, Gallagher," Maslow said.

"Why not?"

"Take it easy, Dave," Harris said to Maslow. And then to Jim. "I talked with MacNeal day before yesterday. I expect to talk to him again this afternoon."

"Did he say how much longer we'll be here?"

"No," Harris said. "We didn't discuss that."

"But you are going to talk to him today?" Gallagher said.

"That's right. I expect to."

"Then I'd like you to give him a message from me."

"Be glad to," Harris said.

"Tell him," Gallagher said, "that late tomorrow morning, probably around noon, my wife and kids and I are leaving here. If he wants us to come to Washington, we'll do that. If not, we're going home to California."

"Well," Harris said, "I don't know if I can give that message to Mr. MacNeal or not. You know, we're responsible for you and your family."

"If you don't want to give him the message," Gallagher said, "that's up to you. But at twelve o'clock tomorrow my family and I are leaving here. Whether you tell MacNeal before we leave or after we've gone is for you to decide."

"Look, we understand how you feel," Maslow said, "but we can't just let you go running off somewhere."

"Never mind how I feel. MacNeal said we'd be here for a week. Or maybe two. It's three weeks tomorrow and we're still here. I wouldn't have come here in the first place if I hadn't been hurt. Now my head's healed up and we're leaving."

"Dave's right," Harris said, "we can't let you go off by yourselves."

"Well, in that case," Gallagher said, "we're going to have an interesting time around here tomorrow morning. Because the only way you'll keep us here is to tie us up. Kids and all. And I don't think MacNeal would like that. Also, if you decide to tie me up, you'd better get yourselves a lot of help." Maslow and Harris exchanged a slow look and Gallagher watched them. Then he said, "I think the best idea is for you to give MacNeal my message when you talk with him today." He turned and walked back down the road to the bridge over the creek. Then on up to the house.

Late that afternoon, Gallagher sat in the side yard with Joannie watching the children make animals out of cucumbers and matchsticks. A car turned in off the road and came down the lane toward the house. He got up and walked to meet it as it slowed down and stopped beside the house. Harris got out and walked over to him. And Maslow who had been reading in the hammock walked over to join them.

"I talked with MacNeal," Harris said. "We'll be leaving the St. Louis airport at noon tomorrow. We should be in Washington not later than three."

■ 3 ■

GALLAGHER AND HARRIS GOT OFF THE ELEVATOR AT THE FIFTH floor and walked left down the corridor to the corner of the building. There they walked through a dark-stained door with the name *MacNeal* printed on it in gold.

Inside his office, MacNeal's intercom buzzed and he pressed the talk button. "Mr. Gallagher is here, sir."

"Fine," MacNeal said. "Send him in." He got up from his chair and walked around to the front of his desk as Gallagher came through the door alone.

"Good morning," MacNeal said. "Come in. It's good to see you."

"It's good to see you," Gallagher said.

"Sit down. Would you like some coffee?"

"No, thanks," Gallagher said, "I just finished breakfast at the hotel."

"We put you at the Buchanan because it's close by," MacNeal said. "I hope your rooms are all right."

"They're fine," Gallagher said.

"How about your family?"

"They're fine, too. We're still not accustomed to having guards outside the door, but otherwise. . . ."

"Nobody ever gets used to that," MacNeal said, sitting down behind his desk. "Even the President chomps at the bit over security. It's good to see you looking so well, Jim. A little better than the last time I saw you in Newark."

"I had a long rest," Jim said.

"Yes, it was longer than we expected. And I can understand your getting impatient. But ever since I saw you, we've been trying to find out exactly what happened to the Torso operation. It's only in the last couple of days that we've had enough information to make sense." He took a cigarette out of a wooden box on his desk and lighted it. "Your head seems to have healed up nicely. What does the doctor say?"

Gallagher smiled. "He says it's healed up nicely."

"Good," MacNeal said. Then, "Well, if you won't have coffee, we'd better get started. You have a busy day ahead of you. In fact, it might stretch into two or three days. Excuse me." He pressed a button on the intercom and waited for an answer light to come on. Then he said, "Walter—Gallagher's here with me. Shall we come in there or do you want to walk over to my office? Fine. See you directly." He turned back to Jim. "That's General Brook. He's an old hand here. He and Wager worked out the whole Torso plan at the beginning."

"Yes, I've heard Burt talk about him," Gallagher said. "They were in North Africa and Italy together."

"That's right." A buzzer sounded then and MacNeal said, "Yes?"

"General Brook is here," a voice said.

"Send him in." MacNeal got up and walked to the door as General Brook entered. "Good morning, Walter. Shake hands with Jim Gallagher. Jim, this is General Brook."

General Brook, a tall, trim man in his sixties, bald on top,

60

with white, close-cropped hair on the sides, suntanned and wearing a neat gray business suit, held out his hand to Jim.

"Good to meet you, Gallagher. How's your head?"

"Pretty good. The doctor says I'll live."

"That's the only medical opinion I know of that's worth a damn. Come on. Let's sit down. Did you have a good flight in from St. Louis?"

"No problems," Gallagher said. "It was fast and straight."

"Harry tells me you got a little impatient with life on the farm."

"That's right. I did."

"I don't blame you a bit. Sorry we had to keep you there so long." He looked at MacNeal. "Well, let's get started. What have you told him, Harry?"

"Nothing much," MacNeal said. "Just that we've been trying to pick up the pieces of Torso."

"That's right," General Brook said to Jim. "We've gone over the whole works. From the time you and Wager and Ramsey went to Berlin three and a half years ago. As you know, there was a lot of material. But we've boiled it down and weeded it out till we got what we think is a history of the whole operation. We've put it on tape."

"Between six and seven hours of listening," MacNeal said.

"And that's exactly what we want you to do," General Brook said. "Listen to the whole damned thing. Listen to it ten times if you want to. And make notes. If there's anything left out or if something on the tape doesn't jibe with the facts as you know them, we want to know about it." He stood up then and took a step toward the door. "So that's it, Gallagher. The quicker you wade through that tape, the quicker the three of us can sit down and chew it over."

Late that afternoon, the sun cooling and falling out of sight behind the government buildings and the fluorescent tubes in the parking lot downstairs beginning to flicker on, Gallagher turned off the tape machine, stood up, walked to the window and looked out. As he turned back to the desk, tightening his necktie and putting on his jacket, there was a quick knock on the door and MacNeal came in.

"How are you getting along?"

"I just finished the last reel," Gallagher said.

"That's fast. I hope you took time off for lunch."

"I had a sandwich and some coffee sent in," Gallagher said.

"Here's the last of my notes. I gave the rest of them to your secretary a couple of hours ago."

"Good," MacNeal said. "I'll have these typed with the others."

"So what's the next step?" Jim said then.

"The next step for you is to go home and have a martini. We won't need you until late tomorrow morning. General Brook and I will hash over this material tonight. Then he and I will get together again first thing tomorrow. We should be ready for you by about eleven. Why don't you plan to come in then?"

■ **4** ■

MACNEAL'S DESK CLOCK SAID THREE O'CLOCK. THREE LUNCH trays piled with dishes, silverware, and napkins were still there in the office, one on the window sill, one on the carpet against the wall, and the other on top of a file cabinet marked *Sealed*. The tape machine stood on a rolling stand at one end of MacNeal's desk, there was smoke hanging in the air, and the ashtrays were filled. MacNeal loosened his tie another inch, pushed his chair back from the desk and said, "All right, Gene." His secretary, a thin young man with frizzy blond hair, picked up his dictation book and several file folders and left the room, closing the door behind him.

MacNeal and General Brook looked at each other. Then MacNeal stood up and walked to the window, lighting a cigarette as he turned and sat on the window sill facing back into the room.

"I still don't believe it," Gallagher said.

"The evidence is all there, Jim," MacNeal said.

"It *seems* to be there," Jim said, "but I knew Ramsey. And that's more evidence to me than all the folders we could stack in this office."

"Of course you knew him," General Brook said. "You knew Ramsey and so did Wager. But sometimes you can't trust what you know. Sometimes you can't believe what you see. You may

62

not realize this, but every time a man goes over the line, every single time one of our men defects, there is always one man or two men or a dozen men who knew him and worked with him and trusted him. Those men, most of them, never do accept the fact that this friend of theirs was a bad apple. Espionage teaches a man some strange lessons. He learns that he can't trust another human being in the world and at the same time he learns that he can't work alone. Someplace between those contradictory facts he has to find a place where he can survive and keep on working. One way to survive is to refuse to believe betrayal until it hits you smack between the eyes."

"The way it hit Wager," MacNeal said.

"And the way it almost hit you," General Brook said.

After a moment, Gallagher said, "Do you think Wager suspected Ramsey?"

"I guess we'll never know that," MacNeal said. "You didn't suspect him. And I doubt if Wager did."

"We admit we don't have a concrete case against Ramsey. We very seldom do have until one of their people comes over to us with facts and figures. It always happens sooner or later, Jim. And it will happen in this case, too. But until it does, we have to base our conclusions on what we know. Wager's dead. If Ramsey didn't kill him, he certainly set him up for it. We know he fed Wager phony information that was supposed to be from Hector and there's not much doubt that Ramsey killed Hector."

"But there is some doubt," Gallagher said.

"Of course there is," MacNeal said. "We can't be absolutely certain he tried to kill you, either, but it seems very likely that he did. He was in the car. He called you over. You recognized his face and his voice."

"But I can't be sure he shot me," Gallagher said. "There was another man in the car with him."

"We know that," MacNeal said, "and we may have a line on who that man was. We've been back-tracking all of Ramsey's movements for the past few weeks and we think we've linked him to a man named Cöswig."

"Who's Cöswig?" Gallagher asked.

"He's a jaybird who's been buying and selling people and information for the past thirty years." General Brook said. "He's treacherous and he's a mean bastard but there always seems to be somebody who's willing to pay for his services. For the last year or so, he's been playing footsie with KGB."

"You say Brian knew him?" Gallagher asked.

"It looks that way," MacNeal said.

"But you don't know for sure?" Gallagher said.

"We were just about to get some hard information," General Brook said, "when somebody opened Cöswig up like a water-melon and left him propped up against the wall outside his apartment building."

"Then you don't know for sure?" Gallagher said.

"We know," MacNeal said, "but we can't prove it."

"Look, Jim," General Brook said, "you're doing what any man would do. Ramsey was your friend and you're trying to give him the benefit of the doubt."

"No, I'm not. I'm not trying to give him anything. But I'm not going to condemn him before I'm sure he's guilty. Maybe he did set up Burt. Maybe they held a gun to his head and forced him. Maybe he set me up, too. Maybe he even shot me. But I'll tell you this much. If Brian wanted to kill me, I'd be dead now. He never missed a target fifteen feet away in his life."

"Whether he pulled the trigger or not doesn't matter, Jim."

"It matters to me," Gallagher said. "If he didn't do *that*, how can I be sure what he *did* do? We're talking about what he might have done. All I can think of are the things I *know* he did. I fought beside him in Korea. So did Wager. We'd both have been dead two or three times if it hadn't been for Ramsey. He was the iceman. He always did the tough jobs." He got up and put on his jacket and walked to the door. "Maybe he did go over to the East. If he did, I guess you'll find out about it sooner or later. But until I know for sure, all I can believe is what I know."

Nearly four hours later, MacNeal sat alone at his desk, sign-ing letters, his secretary standing beside him. General Brook, wearing a lightweight raincoat and carrying his hat, came into the office as the secretary walked back to the outer office.

"Why don't you go home?"

"I am. About ten more minutes," MacNeal said.

"Did you talk to Gallagher?"

"Yeah, I called him at the hotel awhile ago. He's taking his wife out to dinner tonight."

"I think he's a good man, Harry."

"You bet he is," MacNeal said.

"Do you think he'll stick?"

"I don't know," MacNeal said. "He's got a bad taste in his mouth right now. He was Wager's man. Wager brought him

Of All Brands Sold: Lowest tar: 2 mg. "tar," 0.2 mg. nicotine
av. per cigarette, FTC Report Apr. 1976. Kent Golden Lights Menthol:
8 mg. "tar," 0.7 mg. nicotine av. per cigarette by FTC Method.

KENT GOLDEN LIGHTS MENTHOL.
LOWER IN TAR THAN ALL THESE MENTHOL BRANDS.

8 mg. tar,
0.7 mg. nic.

Salem
19 mg. tar,
1.3 mg. nic.

Salem Lights
12 mg. tar,
0.9 mg. nic.

BELAIR
15 mg. tar,
1.1 mg. nic.

KOOL Filter Kings
17 mg. tar,
1.3 mg. nic.

KOOL Milds
13 mg. tar,
0.8 mg. nic.

VANTAGE MENTHOL
11 mg. tar,
0.8 mg. nic.

DORAL MENTHOL
12 mg. tar,
0.8 mg. nic.

Alpine
14 mg. tar,
0.8 mg. nic.

MERIT Menthol
9 mg. tar,
0.7 mg. nic.

REAL MENTHOL REFRESHMENT
AT ONLY 8 MG TAR.

© Lorillard, U.S.A., 1976

Parliament	DORAL	Marlboro LIGHTS	Winston Lights	VANTAGE	MERIT Filter
16 MG TAR 0.9 mg. nic.	**13** MG TAR 0.9 mg. nic.	**13** MG TAR 0.8 mg. nic.	**13** MG TAR 0.9 mg. nic.	**11** MG TAR 0.7 mg. nic.	**9** MG TAR 0.7 mg. nic.

STILL SMOKING MORE TAR THAN YOU HAVE TO TO GET GOOD TASTE?

ONLY 8 mg tar

TASTE KENT GOLDEN LIGHTS.

Of All Brands Sold: Lowest tar: 2 mg. "tar," 0.2 mg. nicotine av. per cigarette, FTC Report Apr. 1976. **Kent Golden Lights:** 8 mg. "tar," 0.7 mg. nicotine av. per cigarette by FTC Method.

Warning: The Surgeon General Has Determined That Cigarette Smoking Is Dangerous to Your Health.

over from G-2 at the same time he conned the British into lending him Ramsey. Without Wager, Jim may not be very interested in staying on."

"It's a helluva mess," General Brook said.

"Yes, and I've got a feeling it's not over yet," MacNeal said.

"What about Security?" General Brook said. "What do they say?"

"Same thing they reported in St. Louis. Gallagher is always under surveillance."

"Familiar faces?"

"No," MacNeal said. "New faces."

"Any chance of lassoing one?"

"Maybe. They're hoping to get hold of one tonight."

■ 5 ■

AT A FEW MINUTES BEFORE EIGHT THAT EVENING, GALLAGHER and Joannie, preceded by Harris, came out of their suite in the Buchanan and walked down the hall toward the elevator. Gallagher was wearing a new dark suit with a blue silk tie and Joannie a black dress trimmed with lace.

As they stood in the descending elevator, Harris checked the other passengers. The gray-haired man with a large stomach was the senior senator from North Dakota. Harris had never seen the woman before but since she was gray-haired, too, and plain, he assumed it was the senator's wife. The third passenger was a nondescript balding fellow in a loose-fitting glen plaid suit and wearing eyeglasses. He looked like a Prudential representative from Peoria.

In the lobby, Harris followed close behind the Gallaghers as they angled across toward the doorway of the main dining room. As he passed Maslow and another man near the cigar counter, he nodded almost imperceptibly toward the man in the plaid suit. As Harris walked on into the dining room with the Gallaghers, the two men closed in on glen plaid from either side and hustled him out through a side entrance.

It was a lovely dining room. Carpeted, elegant, and dimly candle-lit. The waiters, starched and pressed, moved quickly and quietly about and a string orchestra played sensually and softly from a raised area, half-sheltered by camellia blossoms. Gallagher and Joannie were seated in a corner booth opposite the orchestra and Harris, who had left them in the doorway, hurried to join an attractive blonde girl who was already seated at a table fifteen feet away from the Gallaghers' booth.

Outside, in the parking lot, Maslow and the other man squeezed into the back seat of a five-year-old Cadillac with the man in the plaid suit. Maslow leaned forward to whisper something to the driver and as he sat back, the man in the plaid suit slumped over sideways, his mouth open and his eyes rolled back in his head.

Gallagher called the captain over to his table. "Bring us a vodka martini straight up. With an olive. And a Rob Roy on crushed ice."

"And will you order now?"

Gallagher glanced at Joannie and she shook her head. "We're in no hurry," he said. "We'll drink for awhile."

The captain left then and Joannie, looking around the room, said, "Fancy."

"Synthetic," Gallagher said, "but fancy."

"I like it," Joannie said.

"It seems like six months since the last time I took you out to dinner."

"Three weeks and six days."

"It seems like six months," Gallagher said. Then, "I'm going to make a little speech to you. Then we'll forget it. Okay?"

"Okay," she said.

"I can't tell you much about what's been happening."

"I understand that."

"You know that Burt is dead. And Brian may be dead, too, for all I know."

"I'm so sorry, Jim."

"So am I, but sorry doesn't help much. Right now I'm thinking about you. And I'm sorry for the way things have been. I haven't been able to talk with you much these past three weeks. I wanted to but I couldn't. I didn't know what to think. Let alone what to say. I don't even know what to say now."

"Then don't say anything," Joannie said.

The waiter came up then with the drinks. "The martini?" he said.

"For the lady," Gallagher said. The waiter thanked him, put the drinks down and left. ——

"What I'm trying to say is this," Gallagher went on. "It was important to me for you to be there. Seeing you with the kids, watching you move around and talk and be nice to people while I stood off to one side like an invalid."

"Everyone understood, Jim."

"Did you?"

"Yes."

"End of speech," he said, touching his glass to hers.

In the library of General Brook's home in Alexandria, the phone rang. A servant came through the doorway from the hall but General Brook, in a dinner jacket, entering from a door opposite, waved him away. He picked up the receiver and said, "Yes."

"MacNeal, Walter. Can you talk?"

"Yes."

"Security picked up one of those new faces we were talking about."

"Where?"

"At the Buchanan. They spotted him yesterday and they picked him up tonight as he came out of the elevator."

"Where is he now?"

"In the morgue," MacNeal said. "He bit a cyanide capsule as soon as they got him in the car."

"The hell he did. I thought they'd stopped that foolishness."

"So did I. Anyway, we're running a check on his papers and clothes. We don't expect much, but if anything turns up I'll get in touch with you."

Back in the Buchanan dining room, Gallagher was saying, "So that's the way it is. A foreign assignment is out of the question. They've got pictures of me and pictures of you and they probably have footprints of the kids. So—as far as any activity overseas is concerned, I'm dead." Then, "You want another drink?"

"Since you're out of a job, maybe we can't afford it."

"We can afford it." He signaled the waiter for a reorder. Then he said, "They want me to stay on here in Washington."

"What would you be doing?" she asked.

"Some kind of desk job, I guess. It would probably be connected with Far East operations."

"But you wouldn't be going there?" Joannie said.

"Not a chance. They've got my picture up there, too. The world of espionage has a small population." The waiter came with the fresh drinks. "Well, what do you think?" Gallagher said.

"About your taking the job?"

"About the whole idea. Living here in Washington and everything."

"What do you think?" she asked.

"Oh, no," Jim said, "you're not going to side-step me with that one."

Joannie laughed and took a sip from her drink. "Well, gee, I don't know, Jim. I *like* Washington. When we lived here before, I liked it."

"That wasn't quite the same," Gallagher said. "I had only six months to go on my enlistment so we knew it was only for a short time. This would be more permanent."

"That seems like a long time ago, doesn't it?" she said.

"A little over four years and don't change the subject."

"You're relentless, aren't you?" she said.

"Yep."

After a moment she said, "Well, I'm sorry but I can't help you. You'll have to decide for yourself what you want to do and where you want to do it."

"You won't help, huh?"

"That's right, Papa. You have to decide."

"You're playing right into my hands," he said. He smiled and took a drink. "Because I've already decided and I'll tell you what I want. Or rather what I *don't* want." He paused again and looked at her. Then he said, "I don't want to stay on here. As far as I'm concerned, this life is finished. I don't want you or the kids ever to be in a scary or dangerous situation again. Not if I can help it. Does that make sense?"

"Yes," Joannie said.

"If it hadn't been for Wager, I'd never have been in this whole business anyway. So now I think it's time to stop. Am I right?"

"You know what's right for you."

"But what do you think?" he said.

"I think you're right."

"Then that settles it," he said. "Now—since you know what

we're *not* going to do, perhaps you'd like to know what we *are* going to do."

"Let me guess," she said.

"Go ahead."

"I give up."

"It's very simple," he said. "We're going to do what we planned to do in the first place. Before Korea."

"You're kidding," she said.

"No, I'm not. I'm going back to U.C.L.A. and get my master's degree. And in the year and a half or so that that will take, I intend to live with you and the kids in a small house in Santa Monica or Westwood or one of those other slum areas. And I promise you we will have some fun."

"I can't believe it," Joannie said.

"You *can* believe it because it's true," Gallagher said. "And when I get my degree, I'm going to teach school, get fat, and smoke cigars. Do you approve?"

"I approve," she said.

"Good. Now, here's the first step. We will take the kids to your folks in Santa Maria. Then after a few days' visit, you and I, alone like two lovers, will drive down to Santa Monica, live in a hotel, swim on the beach, eat steaks, drink wine, and look for a house for us to move into. Am I brilliant and wise?"

"*Comme toujours,*" she said.

"Does it make you happy?"

"Nothing could make me happier."

"One more thing," he said after a moment. "I can't find any way to figure out for myself what happened in Berlin. And even if I could figure it out, I guess I'd never be able to understand it. So I'm going to try as hard as I can to cut off all that time there and everything that happened. I owe it to you and the kids and I owe it to myself, I guess. We have to put all that away now and find another life for ourselves. Do you understand?"

"Yes," she said.

"Do you agree?"

"Yes," she said. "I agree."

▪ 6 ▪

FOR NINE DAYS THEY CONSUMED SANTA MONICA AND VICINITY.
"Let's squander a little," Jim said. "We deserve it." They
lived at the Miramar in a cottage by the pool. They swam in the
pool and they strolled across the highway and swam in the
ocean. They sat in the sun in their bathing suits and drank
exotic cocktails with fruit floating in them and got high and
laughing and irresponsible in the middle of the day. They ate
dinner at the hotel sometimes. And danced in the tropical
dining room. Or at Jack's-at-the-Beach. Or they drove up the
highway past Malibu to the Holiday House. They went to bed
late and got up early and collapsed in their bed after lunch
every day for a nap. "We need our rest," Joannie said. After the
first three days she wrote it on the dresser mirror with lipstick.
But the tempo didn't slow down. And somehow, mingled and
intermingled with all this self-willed idiotic choreography, they
found time, made time, to look at houses. Santa Monica was
their choice, they decided. This after a laughing afternoon
ranging the Coast highway from the colony to Zuma beach,
seriously inspecting seventy-thousand-dollar beach homes and
damp, ill-smelling beach shanties on stilts and recently flung
up bachelor apartments with kitchenettes, tiled bathrooms
with jeweled fish set in the plaster, and hide-a-beds in the
living room. "Not for us," Jim said. "Not for Jake and Ellen.
Let's live square and old-fashioned in a square and old-
fashioned neighborhood in tacky and beautiful old Santa
Monica."

They sat in real estate offices a lot and listened to ladies with dyed brown hair and men in drip-dry shirts with bow ties talk about what was needed, what was quite miraculously available and how little it would, miraculously, cost. They were taken to many of these properties for minute inspections and well-rehearsed harangues. Several of them they almost liked, many of them were depressing, and one they fell in love with but could not afford. At last, without benefit of realtors, while on their way to Beverly Hills one afternoon, Joannie said, "Hey, there's a house." There was indeed a house. It was for rent and they loved it even more than the house they could not afford. This one they could afford and they signed the lease that evening.

Three days then with the Okadas at their ranch home near Santa Maria. The children spoiled and overindulged now and running big-eyed through the cool hallways and hiding in the abundance of rooms. Hide-and-seeking in the gardens and the implement buildings and spilling food from their chopsticks. "Wait till we get you home," Joannie said to Jake, "the boom will fall. "Boom-boom," Jake said and ran off after his sister, his grandfather on his short legs laughingly and overindulgingly running along behind.

"Are there many closets?" Mrs. Okada said on the last evening as she helped her daughter pack the children's new clothes into two large bags.

"Plenty," Joannie said. "It's an older house, as I told you. Spanish style. But the inside has all been redone. All three bedrooms have sliding-door closets. There's a big hall closet downstairs and a storage closet upstairs. Besides a tremendous linen closet."

"Is there a basement?"

"Yes. It's been paneled and it has a tile floor and it's very dry. It will be good for the kids to play in when the weather's bad outside."

Mrs. Okada wondered if she would put a washer and dryer down there in the basement.

"No," Joannie said. "There's a new laundry room just behind the kitchen. All white and clean with a big double sink. And there's a half-bath there too."

Mrs. Okada said it sounded very nice. "You're lucky to find such a nice place."

"We're very lucky," Joannie said. "We're lucky all right."

▪ 7 ▪

THERE WAS NO FLAW IN THE HOUSE. IT SUITED THEM PER-
fectly. And it pleased them. All four of them. Only the barbecue
in the fenced backyard seemed a disappointment.

"The darned thing just won't work," Joannie said, sometime
in the second week, after a lot of smoky experiments resulting
in unusual dinners.

"Maybe it's me," Jim said. "I must be doing something
wrong."

"It's not you, darling. There's something wrong with *it*."

"It smokes, Daddy," Jake said.

"I suspect it's me," Jim said. "I will keep trying."

They had lived in the house for several weeks, almost five,
before the conflict between Gallagher and the barbecue began
to resolve itself. By this time he had registered at Westwood,
pre-registration, and had preliminary talks with the Oriental
languages department head about his graduate work. The
house was furnished and stocked and functioning smoothly and
the children had settled in, at least partially recovered from the
surfeit of love that had been spooned into them by their
grandparents. Only the barbecue remained stubborn and
uncooperative.

Then one early evening in August, even the barbecue came
around and began to mesh with all the benevolent, surrounding
gears. The smoking stopped, the charcoal glowed quickly and
brightly and began to send off a steady heat and the
hamburgers cooked and sizzled and browned to crisp
perfection.

72

"Gee, these are good," Joannie said. "Isn't Daddy a good cook, Jake?"

"I guess so," Jake said.

"Thanks, Jake," Gallagher said.

"It's a beautiful barbecue after all," Joannie said.

Gallagher said, "I was just about ready to drop a small grenade inside it and walk away."

"I wasn't worried. I knew you'd win."

"I wasn't that sure," he said.

"Why did it smoke so much at first?" she said.

"I'd rather not discuss it," Jim said. Then, "Eat your food, Jake."

The telephone rang in the kitchen.

"Sit still," Jim said. "I'll get it." He walked across the broad backyard and in through the back door. He picked up the receiver and said hello.

"I'm from Blue-point," a voice said. "There's some news about Torso. I'll be at the ice cream parlor at the corner of Ninth Street and Montana in fifteen minutes. I'll be in the last booth. And I'm wearing a green tie."

Gallagher slowly hung up the phone and stood there against the wall, his hands at his sides. Through the kitchen window he could see the children laughing and wrestling with each other inside their jungle gym.

Gallagher pulled into the parking lot, got out of his car, and walked inside the ice cream parlor. It was air-conditioned and sweet smelling and crowded with teen-agers and a few overcaloried matrons. He stopped by the jukebox just inside the front door and looked across the field of heads bent over ice cream to the back of the room. In the back booth, a man was sitting alone. He was wearing a dark suit and a bright green tie.

As Gallagher sat down in the booth across from him, the man in the green tie closed the magazine he'd been looking at and pushed it to one side. "My name is Woodson," he said. Then, "I keep forgetting your father's name."

"Ralph Mills Gallagher."

"He was a teacher, wasn't he?"

"A minister," Jim said. "He was a Presbyterian missionary in Japan."

"That's right. I keep forgetting. And what was your mother's name again?"

"Alice Revere," Gallagher said.

The waitress came up to them then and Woodson ordered coffee ice cream with chocolate sauce. "And a cup of black coffee," he said.

"Just coffee for me," Gallagher said as the waitress started away.

"I'm normally not much of an ice cream man," Woodson said. "I eat a lot of sea food. Do you know anything about oysters?"

"Not much," Gallagher said. "Do you?"

"Blue point oysters breed in northern latitudes from the end of May until September. And in southern waters from March to December."

"The Japanese oyster," Gallagher said, "was successfully introduced to the Pacific Coast of North America. And to Australia."

Woodson took out a cigarette and lighted it. Then he asked Gallagher how he liked California.

"I like it fine," Gallagher said.

"Have you ever lived here before?"

"Most of my life," Jim said. "My folks sent me here when I was thirteen. I lived with my uncle in Mandeville Canyon."

"What did your uncle do?" Woodson asked.

Gallagher said he was a screen writer.

"Does he still live here?" Woodson asked.

"No. He drank himself to death."

The waitress came then with their order and Jim watched as Woodson ate his ice cream rapidly without saying a word. Then he wiped his mouth, took a sip of coffee, and put one hand on the *Newsweek* magazine he had been looking at earlier.

"There's something in here that might interest you," he said.

He opened the magazine and spread it in front of Gallagher. Jim looked down. On the International Business page, carefully pasted into position as though it was a part of the printed magazine, was a photograph of Brian Ramsey. "Does that interest you?" Woodson asked.

"Yes, it does," Jim said.

"He's here in the States," Woodson said, sipping from his coffee cup again.

"Are you sure?"

"Positive. He came through Veracruz and Laredo. Five days ago."

"What am I supposed to do?" Gallagher said, closing the magazine and handing it back.

74

"We think he's here because of you. We think he came here to kill you." Gallagher started to speak but Woodson held up one finger. "Wait a minute. MacNeal said you would never believe it. But he also said to tell you that things have changed since he saw you in Washington. Now they have facts and figures. Does that mean anything to you?"

"Not till I see them it doesn't," Gallagher said.

"You'll see them. MacNeal will be out here in two or three days."

"All right," Gallagher said. "I'll see him then."

"Gallagher, I know you're not officially connected with us any more. And you never laid eyes on me until you sat down here a few minutes ago. But believe me when I tell you that we're not out here for our health. There's something in the air and the signs indicate that you could get hurt. So listen to me. Cooperate. Don't wait till you see MacNeal. Help us now. And let us help you."

"What do you want me to do?" Gallagher said.

"We want you to stay home. And stay inside the house. And most important, if we get in touch with you and tell you to run, you run! Will you do that?"

"All right," Gallagher said after a long moment. "I don't like it but I'll do it. I'll stay home till MacNeal gets here. But I want to see him the minute he hits town."

"You will," Woodson said. He handed Jim a folded napkin then and said, "Here's the fire-drill number. If anything looks fishy, call us. We won't be far away."

■ 8 ■

"THREE DAYS WON'T BE BAD," GALLAGHER HAD SAID TO Joannie. "We can stand three days."

But even one day was bad. That whole agonizing waiting time in Missouri came back to him. Compounded now. And irritatingly intensified. Worse than before. No fields to prowl in now. No woods or pastures or creek beds to cross. Just walk from one room to the other. Look out the windows. Look at the street, the driveway, the back yard. Play with the impatient-to-be-outside children, lie to them, scold them, eat, sleep, watch television, read the newspaper, reread it, look out the windows and pace the rooms of the house.

Up early. From the first day. The milkman came at five. Gallagher watched him. A medium sized clean-cut young fellow with black curly hair neatly trimmed beneath his white cap. Quick-moving. Anxious to get ahead. Manage the dairy. Own his own dairy perhaps. Then the gardeners came. All over the neighborhood. And children spilled out on lawns and into the streets. Bicycles, wagons, and scooters. And men going to work. Grocery deliveries and women driving out to go shopping. Gardeners clipping and mowing and going back and forth to their trucks at the curb. Coming and going. Deliveries and solicitations. Cars cruising past and speeding past. Screeching tires on the boulevard curve two blocks north. Quiet in the house. The radio off and Joannie quiet in the kitchen and the children sulky and drowsy and confused by their silent father. The dry cleaning is delivered. A television aerial salesman is repulsed quickly. Other doorbell rings get no answer. Dogs bark in the silent midafternoon, the children sleep, Joannie does laundry in the room behind the kitchen and Jim sits in the cool shades-drawn dimness of the living room, caged and angry and wondering.

On the second day, midmorning, Jim went into the kitchen where Joannie was working and said, "Come here a minute." She followed him to the side window of the dining room, looking out on their driveway and side yard and into the twenty-yards-distant side yard of their neighboring house, the neighbors away in Europe but plants still needing attention.

"Isn't that a new gardener next door?" he said. They both looked out through the shades at the tall raw-boned man with gray hair working at the trees with a long-handled limb trimmer.

"I've never seen him before," Joannie said. "He must be new."

"They had a little guy before," Jim said. "Short and fat."

"That's right. He always wore a bright blue shirt."

Jim left the window and walked to a wall phone in the hall leading to the driveway. He dialed a number and stood waiting. Joannie stayed at the window, still watching the gardener.

"Hello, Blue-point. This is Gallagher. No, I don't think so. Everything seems quiet. That's right. I just wanted to tell you there's a new gardener next door." He listened for a moment then went on. "He's a tall man. Gray hair. Looks like a dirt farmer from Arkansas. Uh-huh. All right. I'll talk to you later." He hung up and walked back to Joannie at the window.

"What did they say?" she asked.

"He's on our side."

That afternoon, the milkman, who had made his regular delivery in the morning, came back. He parked his white truck aross the street just opposite Gallagher's front door, strolled up the walk onto the front porch and rang the bell.

"Front door, Mummy," Jake called from the kitchen.

"Shhh. Play quietly." As she walked softly into Jim's den, she said, "It's the milkman."

"Yeah, I know. I saw him come up the walk."

"I wonder what he wants," Joannie said.

Gallagher said, "Maybe he wants to collect."

"We're paid up," Joannie said. "Should I go to the door?"

"Better not," Gallagher said.

The milkman left the door then and crossed back to his truck. He got in behind the wheel, closed the door, and lighted a cigarette. "Nobody came to the door," he said.

From the darkness in the back of the truck, a voice said, "I know. I was watching."

"Now what?" the driver said, looking straight ahead at the street.

"We try again tomorrow."

"Why does he have to come to the door?" the driver asked.

"I want to see him," the voice said. "Give me a cigarette."

The driver passed a pack of cigarettes back into the dimness, turned face front again, and said, "I'm sure he's there."

"I will be sure he's there when I see him come to the door."

■ 9 ■

THE MILK WAS DELIVERED AT FIVE THE FOLLOWING MORNING. And in the middle of the afternoon, just as he had the day before, the milkman came back, walked up on the porch and rang the bell. Joannie looked into the den. Jim shook his head slowly. They listened as the doorbell rang twice more. Then they heard footsteps across the porch and, a moment later, the truck driving away. Gallagher stood up, walked to the phone and said, "Let's find out about the milkman."

Midmorning the next day, Gallagher prowled the house upstairs and down while the children fussed and complained about being kept upstairs until Joannie took them to the playroom in the basement. He sat down at his desk and wrote names and drew stars and circles and a crosshatch of straight lines on the desk blotter. He went to the kitchen for a glass of water. He switched the radio on, then after a moment, switched it off. He walked to the side window of the dining room and stood for a long while watching the gardener next door. At last he walked deliberately to the hall phone, took down the receiver and dialed.

"This is Gallagher. You said MacNeal would be here in two or three days. This is the fourth day. Where is he?"

"I just talked with him," Woodson said. "He'll be in late tonight or first thing tomorrow morning."

After lunch, a bit earlier than on the two previous afternoons, Gallagher, in the kitchen, heard the front door bell. Through the shadows of the dining room and the front hallway he could see a silhouette outside the door. "Once again," he said to Joannie, "the milkman cometh. I'll go."

"Good afternoon," the driver said when Gallagher opened the door. "Are you . . ." he glanced at his route book. "Are you Mr. Gallagher."

"That's right," Jim said.

Inside the milk truck, Ramsey crouched on his knees, his face pressed against a periscopic watching device. In the cross hairs a clear, magnified picture of Gallagher, his lips moving as he spoke with the driver.

"It's a ball-point pen and a notebook for Mrs. Gallagher," the driver said now as he handed over a small gift-wrapped package. "We welcome your business and we hope you'll be happy living here in Santa Monica."

"Thank you," Jim said.

The driver touched his cap and walked back toward his truck. Ramsey kept Gallagher centered in his watching device until he closed the front door of the house.

"All right?" the driver said as he got in the truck.

"All right," Ramsey said. "Everything's all right."

Late that night, in bed, the children asleep long since and the street silent outside, Gallagher, lying on his back, said, "Are you awake?"

"Yes," Joannie said.

"This is a pain in the neck, isn't it?"

"It's not too bad," Joannie said.

"You're much too patient," he said. "I think it's a pain in the neck."

Joannie said it was like a story in a magazine, about people being prisoners in their own house. "It's hard to believe it's happening to us," she said.

"And all because of Brian. Can you believe that?"

"It's hard to," she said. "It' very hard to believe that."

"I can't believe it at all. Can you imagine Brian Ramsey being somewhere in Santa Monica tonight?"

"No, I can't," she said.

"Neither can I."

Fifteen blocks south of them on the corner of Pico and Lincoln Boulevard, a car pulled slowly into the bright neon-lighted driveway of a pink stucco motel. Ramsey and a tall brunette girl got out of the car and the girl walked straight ahead to the office as Ramsey looked at his watch and spoke briefly to the man behind the wheel of the car. The car backed up and pulled out of the driveway then and Ramsey walked slowly ahead to the office.

When he came into the motel room a few minutes later the girl had already begun to undress. Her coat and dress were hanging neatly in the closet, her purse was sitting open on the dressing table and she was now sitting on the edge of the bed peeling off her nylons. Ramsey put a straight chair down at the foot of the bed and sat down to watch her. She draped her stockings over the back of an armchair, then turned to face him and smoothly and deliberately stepped out of her half-slip and panties. Wearing just her brassiere, she walked over then and stood directly in front of him. She put one hand behind her to the brassiere clasp.

"This is what you're waiting to see, isn't it?"

"Yes," he said.

She slipped out of the brassiere and tossed it over to the chair with the nylons. Then she stood calmly in front of him while he stared at her. Her right breast was full and beautiful. Beside it, where the left one should have been, there was a large flat scar, red and angry-looking against her white skin.

"How did it happen?" he asked, never taking his eyes off the scar.

"Didn't they tell you?" she asked.

"Yes. But you tell me."

"I was badly burned. When I was only three years old. Just on this one side. So when I grew up I was short one booby."

He got up from the chair then and, still in his clothes, pulled her down on the bed, pressing his face against the angry scar on her chest.

Gallagher and Joannie are asleep now. Outside the house the air rustles the trees softly and nudges the perfume out of the flowers. A few toys lie scattered in the back yard near the barbecue pit. Gallagher's car sits darkly and silently in the carport at the side of the house. In the street at the foot of the driveway, a car is parked. Inside it, silent and watching, are Woodson and another man. They sit without talking. Occasionally one of them lights a cigarette.

Three-quarters of a mile west, the waves come thumping in heavily on the empty beach. The black of the sky blends with the deep wet black of the water and there's no sound at the edge of the ocean except for the heavy monotonous thump of the waves.

▪ 10 ▪

THE FIRST HAIRLINE OF GRAY LIGHT WAS BEGINNING TO SEPA-rate the sky from the ocean when Ramsey came out of the motel and got into the back seat of the car that was waiting for him. As the car sped away, he began to smear lampblack on his face.

Minutes later, on Gallagher's street, the next-door gardener, his truck hanging with tools and implements on the top and sides, showed up for work. He stood beside his truck and lighted his pipe. Then he ambled across the sidewalk and up the lawn toward the back of the house.

Woodson, watching from the front seat of his own car, said to the man beside him, "There's Tucker. And he's right on the button. Let's go home." The engine came to life softly and the car pulled away from the curb.

At a private airport in Burbank, a silver prop-jet with no markings on the side taxied up to the small terminal building. The door groaned open, the stairs slid into position and MacNeal and Harris climbed down from the plane and hurried into the terminal.

It was almost fifteen minutes now since Tucker had arrived for work. He was smoking his second pipe and walking easily back and forth between his truck and the back yard. Carrying tools he would need for the morning's work. Laying them out in the back yard. Along with two or three baskets to hold cuttings from the hedges and plants. Watchful and silent he moved around in the gray predawn light. He stopped then suddenly beside a tall hedge at the side of the house. He relighted his pipe, cupping the match in his hands. Testing it then, he struck another match and puffed more deeply until the smoke began

81

to draw smoothly and scent the air around him. As he brought his hands down and broke the kitchen match in two pieces, a loop of thin wire snaked out from behind the hedge and settled around his throat, tightening and pulling him backward. The shears he had carried under his arm fell to the ground, points down, and stuck there, as Tucker's legs collapsed loosely underneath him and he was dragged silently backward through the hedge.

A moment later, Ramsey, wearing dark trousers and a dark turtleneck sweater, with a seaman's knit cap over his blond hair and his face smudged with lampblack, moved out of the hedge and stood motionless in the shadows. Then, a small satchel under his arm, he moved forward among the plants and flower beds and stepped over the knee-high stone-wall fencing into Gallagher's side yard. He used the trees and the shadows so well that even alert eyes would have had difficulty seeing him as he moved forward across the broad side yard to Gallagher's house.

At a filling station just off Ventura Boulevard in the valley, Harris came out of a telephone booth and hurried over to the car where MacNeal was waiting. He got in behind the wheel, started the engine and pulled out into the in-bound traffic.

"He'll meet us at San Vicente and Montana. Then he'll take us straight to Gallagher's house. It's not far from there," he said.

"How do things look?" MacNeal asked.

"Peaceful. Tucker just came on twenty minutes ago."

"Good. The quieter the better," MacNeal said.

On Second Street in Santa Monica, three blocks north of the Miramar, Woodson and a tall man wearing a gray suit came out of a white frame house, got into a car parked at the curb, and turned east on Montana.

In front of Gallagher's house, the milk truck pulled up and stopped. The driver got out and walked to the front porch with two quarts of milk. He set them down, walked back to his truck and drove slowly toward the next house. Eyes straight on the street, he said "Are you there?" And in the back of the truck, Ramsey's voice said, "I'm here. Let's find a phone booth."

Inside Gallagher's house everything was still. And dark. Ellen lay curled in her crib with her arms around a stuffed toy.

Jake, bare feet sticking out of the blankets, lay sprawled face down on his bed, sleeping soundly.

Down the hall, in their parents' room, the telephone rang. Jim rolled over, shook himself awake, and picked up the receiver before the third ring.

"Yeah," he said. Joannie raised up on one elbow, watching him.

"This is Blue-point. Move out now," the voice on the telephone said. "Repeat. Move out *now*. Drive straight up the coast highway to the Holiday House. Pull in there and wait in the parking lot. *Move*."

As Jim hung up the receiver, Joannie said, "What is it?"

He swung his legs out of the bed, stood up and started to take off his pajama jacket. "Bundle up the kids," he said. "We have to get out of here."

Six blocks away, at the corner of Seventh Street and San Vicente, the milkman came out of a phone booth and got back into his truck.

"All set?" Ramsey said.

"All set," the driver said.

The milk truck made a U-turn then around a boulevard island and headed east on San Vicente toward Beverly Hills.

A mile and a half away, MacNeal's car pulled up to the curb at the corner of San Vicente and Montana. Two men came running over from a Buick parked in a gas station. Woodson got into the back seat with MacNeal. In the front seat, Harris slid over to let the tall gray-suited man drive. As they pulled out from the curb, heading west on San Vicente, the milk truck passed them, heading east.

Inside Gallagher's house, Jim and Joannie, hastily dressed with raincoats over their clothes, Joannie still wearing pajamas under her raincoat, came down the stairs carrying the children. Jake and Ellen, still sleeping, were wrapped in the blankets from their beds. At the wall telephone just inside the side door, Jim stopped and said, "Just a second. Let me try it again." He shifted Jake so he could hold him with his left arm, unhooked the receiver, and dialed a number. Joannie, standing beside him, with tears in her eyes, could hear the busy signal. "It's still busy," Jim said, hanging up. Then, looking at her, "Hey, come on, don't cry," he said.

"I'm scared," Joannie said.

"You're never scared."

"I'm scared now," she said.

As the milk truck screeched around San Vicente curve and headed south, a police car pulled out, red light blinking and started after it.

"Stay off the freeway," Ramsey said. "Turn left on Wilshire."

Outside Gallagher's house, in the driveway under the carport, it was a little lighter now. But it was a gray, cold, dead light, waves of ground fog rolling across the lawn. Jim and Joannie opened the car doors and stretched Jake, still sleeping, on the back seat. Joannie got into the front seat, holding Ellen in her arms. Jim sat in behind the wheel and put the car key in the ignition. He took his hand away from the key then and looked back toward the house.

"What's the matter?" Joannie said.

"I just had a funny feeling . . ." he said.

"What is it?"

"Wait here. I want to try that number once more."

"Hurry up honey," she said. "It's cold out here."

Jim, already halfway out of the car, started to get back in.

"Here," he said, reaching for the key, "I'll start the heater."

"No," Joannie said, sliding over behind the wheel and putting Ellen on the seat beside her. "No, you go ahead. I'll do it."

Jim closed the car door and ran up the steps to the house. Leaving the side door open behind him, he picked up the receiver and began to dial. As he dialed the second digit, the wall slowly buckled and swayed against him and an eye-searing whiteness flashed through the house and the driveway and the side yard. And as he fell, still holding the phone, under the weight of the wall, with glass and wood flying in from outside, the sound of the explosion in the driveway was full and sickening in his ears.

■ 11 ■

PIECES OF STUCCO AND TIMBER AND GLASS WERE STILL FALLING in the yard when MacNeal's car turned in and stopped at the bottom of the driveway. Woodson and Harris and the driver exploded out of the car running toward the house. MacNeal was already talking on the radiotelephone in the back seat.

A mile east of the San Vicente turnoff, the milk truck, going seventy miles an hour down Wilshire with the police car close behind, sideswiped an approaching car—a red Thunderbird—on a curve and scraping and bouncing and twisting along a line of parked cars jumped the curbing, and slid across twenty yards of damp lawn into a thick hedge. The Thunderbird, out of control, spun out across the center line, made a full, skidding circle and smashed head-on into the police car.

Ramsey, bruised and dazed, but conscious, his left leg dragging behind him, pulled himself out of the back of the truck and around to the side by the driver, who lay sprawled unconscious in the front seat. Glancing quickly at the street behind him, Ramsey took a revolver, silencer in place, from a shoulder holster, pressed it against the base of the driver's skull, and pulled the trigger.

At the curb, a black Chevrolet pulled up and stopped. A man in a checked suit and a bow necktie was getting out as Ramsey hopped and limped and dragged himself over to him.

"Can you get me to a hospital?" Ramsey said, leaning against the side of the car. "My leg's broken."

85

"Hadn't we better wait for the police," the man said. "I'm sure they'll be along in a minute."

Ramsey pulled the revolver out of his pocket and jammed it into the man's stomach. "Get in this car, you son-of-a-bitch, and start driving."

Ramsey pulled himself into the back seat and held the gun against the back of the man's neck. "Go down Wilshire to Santa Monica. Then turn right till you get to the San Diego Freeway. And if we get stopped, you're dead."

MacNeal on the radiophone. "Hello, Blue-point. MacNeal here. Gallagher's house just got hit. Get the Santa Monica police and the State police at once. Repeat. At once. I want a solid wall of men around this property in ten minutes. Then get me General Brook in Washington and Governor Brown in Sacramento. Get on it." He got out of the car then and ran up the driveway toward the house.

Later, not much later, only forty-five minutes, still gray damp morning, less than full light, there were policemen at ten-foot intervals all around the perimeter of the lot where Gallagher's house sat. An eight-foot canvas fence had been quickly strung up around the entire yard. The people in the adjoining houses had been evacuated fifteen minutes earlier, the block closed off to all automobile and pedestrian traffic. At a few minutes after six, two ambulances, curtains drawn, pulled out of the driveway. As they turned right, picked up a four-man motorcycle escort, and drove away, the canvas gate in the closely patrolled canvas fence closed behind them and nothing at all inside the entire enclosure, except for the tops of trees, was visible from the street.

The Polish freighter had been anchored three miles off Long Beach since midnight the night before. A double watch had been posted all night. Now, since dawn, the captain and his mate had stood on the bridge, drinking coffee and looking off toward the coast with binoculars. It was nearly eight in the morning when they sighted the launch. The sea was calm and the launch came smoothly and directly toward the freighter. The captain ordered a chair seat to be lowered and the blond man who was lifted aboard was in the ship's infirmary, his broken leg being prepared for setting, before the launch that had brought him, returning now to Long Beach, was out of sight.

■ 12 ■

THREE DAYS LATER, STEVE OKADA, A JUNIOR EXECUTIVE IN A
bank in Salinas, home now with his family in Santa Maria since
the morning telephone call earlier in the week had brought him
there, backed his father's black Chrysler out of the garage and
stopped it in the driveway in front of the house. His parents
came out the front door then, dressed in dark clothes, and came
down the walk to the car. Steve helped them into the back seat,
closed the doors, got back in himself and started the
heartbreaking drive down the coast highway to Santa Monica.

That night, MacNeal, in his shirt sleeves, stood in a bedroom
of the white frame headquarters house in Santa Monica, a
scotch and soda in one hand, the phone held against his ear
with the other. "That's right, Walter. I think we'll be on
schedule. The lab people will finish up at the house tonight and
we'll be out of there first thing tomorrow morning. Yes, I told
the police commissioner he could release the story as soon as
we're out. That's right. We plan to leave for Washington
tomorrow afternoon."

Next morning at eight o'clock, MacNeal, smoking a cigarette
and looking tired, sat in the back seat of a car heading toward
Hollywood on Sunset Boulevard. As they started down the long
hill toward the U.C.L.A.-Westwood turnoff, he said to Harris
who was driving, "Is he back there?" And Harris said, "Yes.
They fell in about a quarter of a mile back."

At the stop light, Woodson got out of the following car,

walked quickly up to MacNeal's car, and got into the back seat beside him. When the light changed, Harris drove straight ahead on Sunset but the following car turned right into Westwood.

"Any problems?" MacNeal said.

"Nope. When we left, the carpenters were already there starting to work."

"And a few newspapermen, I'll bet."

"No," Woodson said. "They got a surprise. The landlord decided to keep that canvas fence up till he finishes the work. He's got four or five private security cops patrolling it."

"There'll be some mad reporters in this town."

"Yes, I guess so."

MacNeal leaned forward to Harris and said, "Put on the radio, will you, Ralph." Then back to Woodson, "I called the commissioner at home about ten minutes ago and told him he could release the story. It should be on the radio pretty soon now." Music came up on the radio then.

"The papers won't like that much either."

"I guess not," MacNeal said, "but this is Los Angeles. They'll have a new scandal before noon." The music stopped abruptly then on the radio. "Turn it up a little, Ralph."

"We have a report just released about that explosion four days ago in Santa Monica. Let's go to the newsroom and Charles Wader. . . ."

"Tuesday morning of this week, there was a mysterious explosion in a residential section of Santa Monica," Charles Wader said. "Since then, the lid has been on. Police patrols, a fence around the property, and no interviews at all to newsmen. This morning, however, about eight minutes ago to be exact, our reporter at the Police Commissioner's office was handed the following news release. I will read it verbatim. 'Four people were killed in Santa Monica early Tuesday morning when an explosion destroyed their automobile, the carport and one side of the house. The house located at 7612 Palm View Boulevard is owned by a Mr. Steven Elden of Palm Springs. The dead were James Gallagher, 33, enrolled as a graduate student at U.C.L.A., his wife Joan, 33, and their two children, Jake, age four, and Ellen, age two.' That is the entire story as released this morning by the authorities. A tragic accident in which an entire family lost their lives. Those are the facts as we know them. But the mystery remains."

Forty minutes later, MacNeal's car pulled up in front of the wrought-iron gate of a walled estate in Encino. Harris touched a switch on the dashboard and the gate swung open, closing behind them as they rolled through and up the curving driveway to the side door of a rambling English country type home, sitting on a rise overlooking the lawns and gardens.

As MacNeal came into the carpeted foyer, a young man with straight, dark features and early-gray hair came forward through the hallway to meet him.

"I heard the radio report," he said.

"Yeah. Can you wrap everything up by late afternoon?" MacNeal asked him.

"No problem. I'll have everything ready."

"How are things here?" MacNeal asked then.

"Silent."

"Quiet or silent?" MacNeal said.

"Dead silent. Silent as the grave."

"That doesn't surprise me," MacNeal said.

"You want to check?"

"Yes, I do," MacNeal said. He walked over toward the stairs, then turned back. "Ralph and Woodson will be right in. They just took the car around." He started up the stairs as a door closed somewhere in the back of the house. "There they are now," MacNeal said.

At the top of the stairs, MacNeal turned right and walked down a long hallway. He paused then for a moment outside the last doorway on the left at the end of the hall. Then he knocked lightly, opened the door and went in, closing it behind him. He stood with his back to the door, looking into the room, and said nothing. At last he said, "Well, now it's official."

Across the room, a man stood with his back to the door, looking out a wide window at the grounds below. He half-turned now, wearing a bathrobe over pajamas, his arm in a black sling, and looked at MacNeal.

"You're officially dead now, Jim. We released the story."

Gallagher studied MacNeal's face for a long moment, then turned back again to the window.

▪ 13 ▪

LATE IN THE AFTERNOON, IN A COUNTRY CEMETERY OUTSIDE Santa Maria, Mr. and Mrs. Okada and their son and all their relatives and most of their friends and many of Joannie's friends from Berkeley stood quietly around four open graves, four coffins resting on white straps waiting to be lowered. Two large coffins, two very small, one on either side of the two large ones.

Just at that moment, the jet that had brought MacNeal to California was climbing steeply above Los Angeles making a wide circling turn over the ocean and heading away from the sun toward the east. MacNeal and Harris and Woodson sat in the back of the plane, each sitting separately. Smoking or looking at magazines. Up forward in the first seat on the left, Gallagher sat by himself, looking out the window as Los Angeles whirled below, then the ocean, then pieces of the city again, then the desert. There were no tears in his eyes as he stared blankly out at the white emptiness of the sky. There was no expression on his face at all. But at that moment, someplace in the tearless depths of him, the plan began. Or if not the plan itself, at least a seed that would become at last the beginning of the plan.

■ 14 ■

GENERAL BROOK SAT SOLIDLY BEHIND HIS DESK, MACNEAL across from him in a deep leather chair. A male secretary in a gray-green suit tapped out a steady, almost inaudible rhythm on the stenotype machine as Woodson, collar open and tie loosened, talked. In a chair by the window Gallagher sat. Listening. But looking mostly at the gray Washington sky outside.

"The charge went off when we were less than a block away," Woodson said. "The timbers and debris were still falling when we pulled up in front of the house. We had to work fast. Fortunately, it wasn't full light yet. As soon as we found Gallagher and saw that he was alive, we wrapped him in a window drape and hustled him out to the car. Then I scouted the neighborhood for Tucker while Harris and MacNeal checked on Mrs. Gallagher and the children."

"There was nothing we could do for them," MacNeal said. He was aware of Jim as he said it. He looked at him. But Jim's eyes didn't move from the window.

"I found Tucker in the shrubs next door where they'd left him. Then we took off," Woodson said.

"It seemed like an hour, but I think we had Gallagher out of there in seven or eight minutes," MacNeal said.

"Was that when you called me?" General Brook asked.

"That's when I got through to you. When we got back to Woodson's cover house in Santa Monica."

There was a lull, then. The men in the room were specifically

91

aware of Gallagher at the window but he seemed strangely unaware of them. Almost absent. General Brook swiveled his chair around so that he faced Jim more directly.

"It was my decision, Jim," he said finally. "Not the original action when they carried you away from the house. But the ultimate decision about procedure was mine. It was a chance we couldn't pass up. If Ramsey thought he'd killed you, it was important to us that he go on thinking it. Important for KGB to go on thinking it." Gallagher said nothing and General Brook looked at MacNeal.

"After you left Washington to go to California," MacNeal said, "we got new information on Ramsey, stuff we didn't have before. We found out that KGB had big plans for him. But they wanted to be 100% sure of their man. He had to pass the test. First by killing Wager. Then you. When he missed you in Berlin, they sent him here to finish the job. If KGB had found out he'd missed you the second time around, that would have been the end of Ramsey as far as they are concerned. They knew Ramsey had been with us, so if he was going over they wanted to make sure it was all the way. They're scared stiff of double agents."

"And they should be," General Brook said, "because that's exactly what we plan to make of Ramsey. We want to turn him around."

"And we'll do it," MacNeal said.

"Now that he's really sold himself to KGB," General Brook said, "he can be very important to us."

Gallagher turned his head from the window now, stubbed out his cigarette in an ashtray and said, "But only if I'm dead. Is that it?"

"Only if they're *convinced* you're dead," MacNeal said. "And now they will be convinced."

"It was necessary, Jim," General Brook said. "It was a necessary tactical move. It had to be done."

"You really think you got away with it?" Gallagher asked.

"You bet we did," MacNeal said.

"The orders came down from the top," Woodson said. "The Governor knew what was happening. So did the Los Angeles Police Commissioner. They took care of the coroner's office. All anybody else knew was that there had been an explosion and four people were killed."

Gallagher walked around behind the stenotype machine and stood for a moment looking down at the flat black keys.

"And Tucker took my place?" he said then. "Right?"

"That's right," Woodson said. "I carried him into the house as they carried you out to the car."

Gallagher walked to the window again and stood with his back to the room. "Gentlemen," he said finally, "you're in a nice business."

MacNeal cleared his throat and looked at General Brook. Woodson bit the end off a thin, dark cigar and lighted it.

"Jim, I want to tell you something," General Brook said then. "I would give anything I own or ever will own to wipe out what's happened to you. I have children of my own. So does Harry. Just because we don't talk about how we feel doesn't mean we don't have feelings. You're right about this business. It's a mess. And it gets messier all the time. There's no logic in it and no decency. It's stop-and-start, cut-and-paste. And sometimes it's kill or be killed. It's lousy but nobody's ever found a way to make it different or better. When I look at my wife and kids and think about what happened to yours, I get sick to my stomach. But once I walk into this building, I can't let myself feel that way. There's no time here for emotion. Or for thinking about how things might have been. All that matters is what *is*. Our game is information. We get it and use it and try to hide it so no one else will get it. Information, Jim. Nothing else."

"You know what it's like," MacNeal said. "You've been a soldier and you've been an agent. And either way it's dirty war. Anybody who fights takes a chance of being killed."

"What about the people who don't fight," Gallagher said. "What about the people who aren't in the war at all?"

"Sometimes they get killed too," MacNeal said.

Driving home that afternoon in MacNeal's car, Gallagher said, "What does a dead man do with himself?"

"That depends," MacNeal said. "Do you have any ideas?"

"Only one. I don't plan to stay in your guest room forever."

MacNeal said, "Do you want a job with us again?"

Gallagher said he thought that was out of the question and MacNeal said perhaps something could, after all, be worked out. "It would have to be something special that would fit the circumstances."

"Like haunting a house?"

"That's a thought," MacNeal said.

"I want to go back to Berlin," Gallagher said then.

"I know you do. But that really is out of the question."

"Why?" Gallagher said. "I'll need a new name and a new passport no matter what I do. So why not Germany?"

"We can't do it, Jim. Even if it were safe for you, which it isn't, it could wreck our whole plan as far as Ramsey's concerned."

They rode along in silence for several blocks. Then Gallagher said, "There are other outfits, you know. *Gehlen* could use me."

"*Gehlen* won't touch you if we tell them not to. And none of the other organizations will either." Then, "Why does it have to be Germany?"

Gallagher said it was just an idea he had.

"Do you want revenge?" MacNeal asked. "Is that it?"

"Maybe."

"On Ramsey?"

"Maybe," Gallagher said.

"You read the whole file on him but you're still not convinced."

"I'm convinced he's a Communist," Gallagher said. "But I'm not convinced he killed Wager. I'm not convinced he tried to kill me and I'm not convinced he planted the bomb in my car in California."

"Don't you think the KGB is behind Ramsey? Don't you think they're behind all this?"

"Sure I do," Gallagher said. "I'm no fool. But that doesn't mean that I'm ready to strap Brian into the electric chair and throw the switch. Politics is one thing and murder is something else."

MacNeal asked him what it would take to convince him and Gallagher said he didn't know for sure. "If anyone had seen him it would be different. I know he was spotted in Veracruz and Laredo. But that's a long way from California."

MacNeal said, "Would a photograph convince you?"

"What do you mean?" Gallagher said.

"I mean that if we showed you a photograph of Ramsey in your yard in Santa Monica, would that convince you that he did everything we say he did?"

"What are you driving at?" Gallagher said.

"Tucker planted half-a-dozen cameras around the outside of your house. We found five of them intact."

"Any pictures?"

"No," MacNeal said, "but there's still a chance with number six. We found parts of that sixth camera in the debris of your car and carport. If we're lucky, there may be some exposed film somewhere in that litter. And if we're really lucky there might be a face on it."

"Ramsey's face?" Gallagher asked.

"Could be," MacNeal said.

■ **15** ■

THAT NIGHT, AFTER MACNEAL AND HIS WIFE HAD GONE TO sleep, Gallagher lay fully dressed on his bed, looking up at the ceiling, his hands behind his head. It was nearly three in the morning when he got up, undressed and went to bed. He went to sleep at once.

The next morning he had breakfast early and alone in the garden. Then he walked to the little lattice summer house and sat there for a long time in a sling chair. From time to time, he scribbled a notation on a folded piece of paper which he refolded each time and returned to his shirt pocket.

Shortly before lunch, he borrowed a portable typewriter from Jane MacNeal, took it up to his bedroom and typed diligently for forty-five minutes. He then folded the original and two carbons, put each copy in a separate envelope and put all three envelopes into his inside jacket pocket.

"You should see the National Gallery while you have some free time," Jane MacNeal said at lunch.

"That's true, I should," Gallagher said. "I'll go this afternoon."

At two o'clock that afternoon, wearing sunglasses and a wilted Panama hat long since discarded by Harry MacNeal, Gallagher walked briskly along through the business streets of Washington. Once or twice he referred to an address he had written on a small card which he carried in his jacket pocket. At last he stopped, checked the address again, and walked into the cool brightness of a glass and aluminum office building. Taking the elevator to the seventeenth floor, he walked down a long corridor and turned through a frosted-glass double door into a carpeted, comfortable but conservative reception room. A middle-aged, no-nonsense receptionist looked up at him as he approached her station.

"My name is Kellogg," Gallagher said. "I have an appointment with Mr. Compton."

"He's on the telephone. If you'd care to sit down for a moment, he'll be right with you."

General Brook at the telephone in his office. "Yes," he said, "you heard me. I want that courier met and isolated before he steps off the plane. Seal his dispatch case and mark it for my eyes only. And I want it here immediately. You understand?" Hanging up, he pressed a button on his intercom and said, "Harry, can you come in for a minute?"

"Be right there," MacNeal said. As he passed his secretary in the outside office, he said, "I'll be in General Brook's office. If that California call comes through, put it in there."

As MacNeal came into his office, General Brook, on the telephone again, said "Sit down, Harry. I'll be right with you."

The receptionist hung up her telephone receiver, stretched her mouth in an almost smile in Gallagher's general direction, her eyes focused on a spot eighteen inches above his head, and said, "Mr. Compton will see you now."

"As you probably heard," General Brook said to MacNeal, "that was my daughter. She refuses to write letters but she calls me once a week."

"Collect," MacNeal said.

"How did you know?" General Brook asked.

"My sons won't write letters either."

His intercom buzzed and General Brook picked up the receiver. "No," he said after listening for a moment. "I don't think that's a good idea. Tell him I'll talk to him at four o'clock this afternoon. And hold my calls until I tell you."

"I'm expecting a California call," MacNeal said quickly. "I told them to put it through here."

"If there's a call for MacNeal," General Brook said into the intercom, "put it through. But hold everything else." Turning back to MacNeal he said, "Did Ruggero come up with something?"

"I hope so," MacNeal said. "I talked with him earlier and he said he'd had a call from the lab. They sifted through the last of

96

the debris from Gallagher's house and apparently they've found some scraps that look like pieces of film."

"Keep your fingers crossed," General Brook said.

"I am," MacNeal said. "Ruggero was leaving for the lab when I talked to him before. He said he'd call me from there."

"Well, this may turn out to be a good day. I called you in here to tell you there's a courier on his way from Berlin. He's supposed to have something hot about Ramsey."

MacNeal asked when he was due to arrive and General Brook said most anytime now. "We should have the dispatch in our hands not later than four. Maybe that's your call," he said as the intercom buzzed and he picked up the receiver. "Yeah? Yeah? Good. Put it on number three." He pointed to a phone on his desk and MacNeal picked it up.

"Hello. Yes, this is MacNeal. Hello. Yeah, Vince, what's the story?"

Mr. Compton, wearing pince-nez, erect, and staying slim in his sixties, walked out through the reception area with Gallagher and shook his hand at the door. Jim, glasses and hat in place, went down in the elevator and back onto the bright sidewalk. He walked only a block and a half this time. When he stopped he went into a bank, all granite and polished brass and uniformed guards with gray sideburns under their caps. He waited in an open enclosure studded with heavy desks for perhaps five minutes, then he was ushered out of sight to another plateau of authority behind oak doors.

The bank had closed and locked its revolving doors when Gallagher came back out into the main promenade. He was let out a side door. As soon as he was in the street again, he took an addressed and stamped envelope from his pocket, dropped a small key inside it, sealed it, and strolling to the closest intersection, dropped it into a bright red and blue letterbox just as the post-office truck arrived with canvas bags to empty out the mail. As the man unlocked the mailbox and began scooping out the cards and letters, Gallagher stepped to the curb and got aboard a city bus that would take him within two blocks of the National Gallery.

▪ 16 ▪

JANE MACNEAL, GRAY-HAIRED AND SUN-TANNED, WITH freckles on her nose contradicting the gray hair, wearing a simple and expensive seersucker dress, looked up from her work, instructing the gardener as he cut fresh flowers for the dinner table, and saw Gallagher walking up the late afternoon driveway. She walked to meet him, cradling a radiant burst of flowers in her bare arms.

"How was the National Gallery?" she said.

"Brilliant," Jim said, walking up to her, "and you look like an early Renoir."

"On behalf of the flowers, I accept the compliment."

"You have quite an armload. You want some help?"

"No thanks. I'm almost finished. You go inside and have a drink with Harry. I'll join you shortly."

"He's home early," Gallagher said.

"Yes, for a change. And I think he's waiting for you."

"All right. I'll go in. See you in a few minutes then."

"Yes," she said, "when I've brushed the thorns and brambles out of my hair."

He found MacNeal in the library, mixing a drink. "Don't scold me," Jim said. "I went out in public today but as you can see I wore my false face."

"Well take off your false face and that dilapidated hat of mine and take a sip of this." He poured a martini, clear and shining, out into a stemmed, frosted glass. He handed it to Jim and poured one, then, for himself. "Jane tells me you went to the National Gallery."

"Yes, I did."

"Any conclusions?"

"Yes," Gallagher said. "I like Gauguin, Cézanne, and Léger."

"How's the drink?"

"Fine. Very good."

"Are you an art connoisseur?" MacNeal asked then.

"Far from it. That's a deficiency in me."

"Me, too, I'm afraid," MacNeal said. "Jane is always quick to point that out. She says very few people know or care to know what the Italian news analysts were saying on the day the Mona Lisa was finished." He waved Jim to a chair and they both sat down. "I think you'd better come down to the office with me tomorrow," MacNeal said. "Things are starting to pop."

"Ramsey?" Gallagher asked.

"That's right. A courier came in today with a hot report from the East Zone. Our people say Ramsey's in Moscow. And this time it's eyeball evidence."

"That didn't take long," Gallagher said.

"We think he got into Mexico City and flew from there to China. Then on into Russia. They say his leg's in a cast and he's using crutches."

"What does that mean?" Gallagher said.

"It all seems to tie in," MacNeal said. "We didn't tell you this before because we weren't sure of the facts ourselves, but the morning that bomb was planted in your car, a milk truck sideswiped a car on Wilshire Boulevard and crashed into somebody's yard. The driver was killed in the crash. Or so the police thought. But when they got him to the morgue, they found a bullet in the back of his head. It turned out to be the milkman who'd been making deliveries to your house."

"Woodson said he was clear."

"We thought he was," MacNeal said. "Anyway, we think Ramsey was in the truck with him when it crashed."

"And that's how he hurt his leg?"

"It makes sense," MacNeal said.

Gallagher asked him how Ramsey got away. MacNeal said he must have flagged a car, stuck a gun in the driver's face and got himself a ride to wherever he was going.

"Tijuana?" Gallagher asked.

"That's what we thought at first," MacNeal said, "but now we think he headed for Long Beach. Last week, the police towed in a car that had been parked near the docks there for several days. When they opened the trunk, there was a man inside. With a bullet in his head. They're comparing the bullet with the one they took out of the milkman. We should have a report in the morning."

Gallagher sipped from his glass. "Is that why you want me to come in?"

"No," MacNeal said. "Something better than that. Remember I told you there was a camera planted in your carport? Well, I talked with the lab in California today and they've found some exposed film. It's in pretty bad shape but they think they can make some prints. They're working on them tonight and they should be in my office tomorrow morning. That's why I want you there."

"I'll be there," Gallagher said.

"Shall I go away and come back later?" Jane MacNeal said, coming into the room from the hallway.

"No. Come in by all means," MacNeal said. "We just finished the shop talk. Now, what would you like to drink?"

She carefully set down a small bowl of flowers she was carrying and said, "Something cold and strong."

Later that night, as they were getting ready for bed, Jane said, "I don't know how he does it. In just a few weeks, he's lost everything. He must be torn up inside."

"Yes, I guess he is," MacNeal said.

"Does he ever talk about it?" she asked.

"Not lately," MacNeal said. "Only once or twice before we left California. He said he couldn't get the memory of those few minutes out of his head, the time right before his car exploded. He kept thinking there was something he could have done to prevent it. He kept saying he should have been smarter."

"Do you think there was anything he could have done?" Jane said.

"No," MacNeal said. "Anyone with Gallagher's training would have done just what he did. He'd been told to run so he was running. The only thing he could do was try to double-check the phone call. That's exactly what he was doing when the car went up."

"I still don't see how he can do it," Jane said after a moment. "How can he manage to stay on his feet and keep it all to himself the way he does?"

"Do you know how they used to cauterize a wound?" MacNeal said.

"Yes."

"That's what Gallagher's done to himself. He's closed it off, seared it shut, and stopped the bleeding. But inside the pain goes on."

"I don't know how he can do it," Jane said. "How can he keep it all inside and smile and have cocktails with us and go to the National Gallery and not show anything to anyone."

"Because he's a man," MacNeal said.

■ 17 ■

"So the puzzle is starting to fall into place," General Brook was saying. "Harry told you what we found out yesterday. Now, this morning, we have two more pieces. The milkman and the dead man in the car trunk in Long Beach were killed by bullets from the same gun."

"What about the pictures?" Gallagher said.

MacNeal said they were on their way in from the airport. "Should be here any minute. Ruggero's bringing them himself."

"Frankly, I think it will be a miracle," General Brook said, "if we find an identifiable face on that film. But for *your* sake, Jim, I hope we do."

"Why for *my* sake, General?"

"Because you're the only one who's still unconvinced. Harry and I and our people in the East Zone are all sure of our man. It's too neat to be wrong. The beginning was in Berlin, the middle was in California, and now we have the end."

"You mean because he's in Moscow," Gallagher said.

"No, that's not what I mean. Tell him the latest report from Germany, Harry."

"You remember," MacNeal said, "that our whole line of investigation on Ramsey was based on the theory that KGB was setting him up for something big. Well, now we know what it is. They're sending him to England."

"It looks as though he'll be one of their key men there,"

101

General Brook said. "It's an important job in an important country. It means they trust Ramsey completely."

"He's proved himself," MacNeal said.

"Unless I'm mistaken," General Brook went on, "he'll be in contact with the top levels of Russian intelligence." The intercom buzzed. "Yes? Fine. Send him right in." He turned back to MacNeal and Gallagher. "It's Ruggero."

The door buzzed and opened and the prematurely gray young man from the estate in Encino came in carrying a black attaché case.

"Hello, Vince," MacNeal said. "Good to see you."

"Hello, Mr. MacNeal."

"You know Jim Gallagher. And this is General Brook. General Brook, Vince Ruggero."

"Good to meet you," General Brook said. "We've been waiting anxiously."

"You should have seen me in that darkroom if you think you're anxious," Ruggero said.

"Did you get anything?" MacNeal asked.

"Yes sir. We got a picture."

"Just one?" MacNeal said.

"That's right," Ruggero said. He started to open the attaché case and the three men moved in behind him. "We only got one. At first I thought there might be something else on the film but it was in such bad shape we were lucky to get anything at all."

"When you got here," General Brook said, "I was just saying that it was a long shot."

"You're right, General," Ruggero said, taking a manila envelope out of the case and starting to unwind the string that closed it. "But I have a hunch maybe this long shot will pay off." He took an 11" x 14" photograph out of the envelope then and put it down on the desk in front of himself and the three other men.

For a long, carved-out moment they all stood staring at the picture. At last MacNeal said, "My God."

The photograph was obviously from a damaged negative. Burned, cracked, and torn around the edges. And several long cracks across it. But clearly and unmistakably in the center, photographed as he lifted the packet of explosives up to the fender of Gallagher's car, was Brian Ramsey, wearing his dark clothes, with lampblack smeared carefully on his face.

"Is that your man?" Ruggero asked.

"That's our man, all right," General Brook said.

Gallagher walked away from the desk and crossed the office to the window. He stood there looking out for a moment. Then he lighted a cigarette. MacNeal watched him.

Ruggero reached into another large envelope and said, "I've got a couple of blowups. If you want to take a closer look at the face."

All three men were aware now of Gallagher at the window. "No, Vince," MacNeal said. "Not right now."

"That's right," General Brook said abruptly, "we can look at the other shots later."

Silently, Ruggero began to put the pictures back into their envelopes. General Brook sat down heavily behind his desk and MacNeal sat in the chair opposite him. Ruggero opened the attaché case to put the envelopes back inside.

Gallagher turned from the window, stubbed out his cigarette in the ashtray and said, "Don't put them away. I'd like to look at them now." He walked over to Ruggero, took the envelope from him, and taking the three enlarged pictures out, set them side by side on a display railing running waist-high along one wall of the room. He stood with his hands in his pockets, his back to the other three men, and stared, long and hard, at the photographs.

■ 18 ■

FORTY MINUTES LATER, GENERAL BROOK CAME OUT OF HIS own office and walked down the corridor to MacNeal's office. MacNeal was behind his desk, Gallagher sitting opposite him.

"I'm sorry to keep you waiting. Those dumb bastards in the State Department should have full-time nurses. Where's Ruggero?"

"He went to take a shower and have some breakfast. I didn't want him here for this meeting anyway," MacNeal said.

"That's right," General Brook said. He sat down in a deep, comfortable chair at the end of MacNeal's desk, and lighted a cigar. "Jim," he said then, "you just saw something happen that's very unusual in our business. We always keep looking for the last piece to the puzzle but we don't usually find it. We usually have to go ahead without it. Trusting our experience, our instinct, and our luck. But not this time. This time we've got a perfect ball-bearing setup. We know the *how*, the *what*, and the *where*. The only thing missing is the *when*. And that can be anytime we want it to be."

"You're talking about turning Ramsey around," Gallagher said. "Right?"

"That's right," General Brook said. "He could become the strongest double agent we've ever had. I suspect that he'll have access to information we've never been able to touch before."

"You know how it works as well as we do, Jim," MacNeal said. "We always get the information we want sooner or later. It's just a question of how long it takes and how many people it has to filter through before it gets to us. If there are too many people we sometimes get the information too late."

"What makes you think Ramsey will be that close to the file cabinet?" Gallagher said.

"Everything points to it, Jim," General Brook said. "And the fact that they're sending him to England clinches it. They've been drifting agents in there for the past eighteen months. They're building up to something big."

"The way it looks now," MacNeal said, "it's something connected with shipping. They seem to be coming and going mostly around the seaports. Liverpool, Newcastle, Cardiff, and the like."

"What if Ramsey won't play ball," Gallagher said. "What if he won't turn around."

"He has no goddamned choice," General Brook said.

"You're the key to the whole thing, Jim," MacNeal said. "The second he finds out you're alive, he'll know his goose is cooked with KGB."

"If he won't work with us," General Brook said. "we leak the word to KGB that you're still alive. Then Ramsey's dead and he knows it."

"We'll give him a few months to get entrenched in England," MacNeal said. "Then we'll move in on him."

"I'm not sure I understand," Gallagher said. "Where do I fit in?"

"As Harry said, you're the key figure," General Brook said. "Everything pivots on you."

"That's funny," Gallagher said, "because ever since things blew up in Germany, I've had the impression that I was a wooden nickel as far as you people are concerned."

"Not now, Jim. You're our ace-in-the-hole."

"Because I'm dead?" Gallagher asked.

"Because you're *not* dead," MacNeal said, "and they think you are."

"This will be the easiest job of your life, Jim. We're going to keep you on ice," General Brook said.

"Where? In MacNeal's guest room?"

"No," MacNeal said, smiling, "and not on that farm out in Missouri either."

"You can pretty much pick your spot," General Brook said. "We've got a place up in Vermont, one in Jamaica, and a lodge out in Colorado near Aspen. Or you name it. You can cruise on a yacht if you want to."

After a moment, Gallagher said, "And what do I do exactly?"

"Nothing," MacNeal said. "You just stay out of circulation till we're ready to move in on Ramsey."

"Then what?" Gallagher said.

"Then," General Brook said, "he'll want some proof that we're not bluffing. That you're still alive. So you may have to write him a letter. We'll take some film of you. Or if he's really hard to convince we might set up a telephone conversation."

"I see," Gallagher said, "and what happens after that?"

"After he's convinced you're alive," MacNeal said, "we have to make sure he doesn't send somebody to do the job he failed to do."

"So I go back into the deep freeze," Gallagher said. "Right?"

"I wouldn't call it that," General Brook said.

"You called it 'keeping me on ice,'" Gallagher said.

"That's right," General Brook said.

"How long do you estimate this exile period would last?"

General Brook said it was pretty hard for him to predict a stop date.

"What do you think, Harry?" Gallagher turned to MacNeal.

"I don't like to make a blind guess," MacNeal said.

"A year? Two years? How about five years?" Gallagher said. "You know, I could become the best gin rummy player in Jamaica. Assuming I had a couple of guards to play cards with. I would have a couple of guards, wouldn't I?"

There was a long silence then. MacNeal got up from his chair and walked over to the window, General Brook chewed on his cigar, and Gallagher sat down in a chair opposite the desk. Finally, MacNeal turned and came back to his armchair.

"Look, Jim," he said, "why not just look at it as a job? It may be dull, but lots of jobs are dull. The main thing is, this particular job is important. *And* you're the only one who can do it." He glanced at General Brook. "And you'll be damned well paid."

"Will I?" Gallagher said. "How much?"

General Brook got up and strolled to the window. "Fifteen thousand a year and we pay all your expenses," he said.

"Is the fifteen thousand tax-free?" Gallagher said.

"If you want it to be," MacNeal said.

"How about a bonus?" Gallagher said.

"You'll get a ten-thousand-dollar bonus," General Brook said.

"Right now or later?" Gallagher said.

"Right now if you want it," MacNeal said.

"And is the bonus tax-free too?" Gallagher said.

"Yes," General Brook said.

"Well," Gallagher said, "that's nice." He sat back in his chair and folded his arms. Then he said, "This must have been under discussion for quite a while. You seem to have the details all worked out."

"There's a lot at stake, Jim," MacNeal said. "We have to work out the details. You know that."

"Yes, I do know that," Gallagher said. He paused a moment and General Brook turned from the window to look at him. "But unfortunately," Gallagher went on, "there's one detail you missed."

"What's that?" General Brook asked.

"I'm not interested," Gallagher said.

"What does that mean, Jim?" MacNeal said.

Gallagher stood up, paced to the wall, then back behind his chair. "It means I'm not interested. I don't want to be put on ice or deep frozen or nailed up in a lodge in Colorado. I don't want a bonus and I don't want a salary. Tax-free or not. I don't want anything to do with the whole arrangement."

MacNeal looked slowly at General Brook. Then he said, "Look, Jim. I guess this came at you pretty fast. We don't have to decide everything right this minute."

"Yes, we do," Gallagher said. "It's already decided."

General Brook came back to his chair then and said the money was open for discussion in case it wasn't satisfactory.

"All right," Gallagher said, "maybe we should discuss the

money. What's the going rate for staying dead and then coming to life on cue?"

"Now, wait a minute, Jim," MacNeal said.

General Brook stood up and twisted his cigar out in the ashtray. "Let me handle this, Harry." he said. Turning slowly to Gallagher, he said, "Now you listen to me, young man."

"No," Jim said, "you listen to me. And don't talk to me as if I'm working for you. I used to but I don't any more. So don't you forget that. Ever since I left Berlin in the middle of the night, you people have been pushing me around like a domino. Go here. Go there. Do this. Do that. Sit up. Play dead. I know your intentions were good. Everything you do is done for a good reason. I know that. But your reasons are not the same as mine. Not any more."

"Jim," General Brook said, "I can understand exactly how you feel. . . ."

"No you can't. You may understand how you would feel if you were in my shoes but you don't know how *I* feel. I'm not even sure myself. Anyway, how I feel doesn't matter. What does matter is what I'm going to do. And that I'm sure about. I'm going to England or Germany or Portugal or Singapore if I have to and I'm going to find Ramsey. And I'm going on my own. For *me*. Not for you or NATO or Blue-point or the star-spangled banner."

"What good will that do, Jim?" MacNeal said after a moment.

"I don't know for sure but I'm going to find out. A few weeks ago I had a wife and two kids and two friends who were like brothers to me. Now, all of a sudden, there's nobody left but me. I don't know what the hell hit me or why but I'm going to find out."

"Gallagher, " General Brook said slowly, "do you remember when I said to you that there's no place in this building for emotion? That wasn't completely true. Naturally, we all have emotional hang-ups. But we can't let that influence our decisions. And that's what you're doing."

"It's easy to understand what you want to do, Jim, and why you want to do it," MacNeal said, "but you have to understand our position, too. You have to understand that we can't *let* you do it."

"I understand that," Gallagher said, "but I don't think you can stop me."

"Of course we can stop you," General Brook said. "We can pick up your passport."

"I don't have a passport," Gallagher said. "Gallagher had a passport but he's dead. Remember?"

"That's my point," General Brook said. "Without a passport, I think you'd find it a little difficult to leave the country."

"General Brook, I worked in intelligence for over five years. Let me ask you a question. Do you know where a man can buy a forged passport?"

"Of course I do," General Brook said.

"Well, so do I. I know two places within a ten-minute taxi ride of this building. And I know half a dozen in New York."

"I think we're missing the main point here," MacNeal said then. "As Walter explained, this Ramsey affair is a big opportunity for us to get an inside look at Russian intelligence. We can't let you do anything to jeopardize that, Jim."

"The only way you can stop me," Gallagher said, "is to lock me up."

"You understand our situation," General Brook said, "and you understand your part in it. It's a very crucial part."

"That means you would lock me up?" Gallagher said.

"I don't like that expression," General Brook said, "but if we must detain you to guarantee the success of this operation, then we have no choice."

"You know, it's a funny thing," Gallagher said. "I had an idea that's what you'd say." He took a long envelope from his inside jacket pocket, took out a sheet of folded paper, carefully unfolded it, and handed it to General Brook. "Here," he said, "I'd like you to take a look at this."

General Brook took the sheet of paper, a questioning look in his eyes. He read it carefully down to the bottom of the page. Then, without looking up, he read it through again.

"Now let Harry read it," Gallagher said, taking the paper and handing it to MacNeal. As MacNeal read, General Brook looked down at his hands and slowly turned his wedding ring around his finger. MacNeal finished then and looked up, first at General Brook, then at Gallagher.

"Now," Gallagher said, "you've both read it. So let me ask you a question. If that story appeared in Alsop's column tomorrow, what would it do to your plans for Ramsey?"

"You won't get away with this, Gallagher," Brook said.

"What would it do, Harry?" Gallagher asked again.

108

"You know what it would do," MacNeal said. "It would wreck the whole plan."

"Why?" Gallagher said.

"Why? Because you've told the whole story of what happened to you in Santa Monica."

"That's right," Gallagher said. "I just wanted to be sure we're all thinking along the same lines."

"And if we don't go along with *your* plan to track down Ramsey yourself," General Brook said, "you'll give this story to the newspapers. Is that correct?"

"Something like that," Gallagher said.

"It's an old trick, Jim," MacNeal said then, "but there's a hitch to it as far as you're concerned. If we have you incommunicado somewhere, you can't very well plant this in the papers, can you?"

"No, I can't," Gallagher said. "But you see, I didn't use the *old* trick. I used a new one. Starting yesterday afternoon, if I am incommunicado for one week, that story will automatically be released to the newspapers." He paused for a moment, then went on. "I did go to the National Gallery yesterday, Harry, but I also made another stop. I put another copy of this story in an envelope, sealed, stamped, and addressed, and left it with a reliable person. Every week this man will receive a postcard from me. If for any reason I am unable to send him that weekly card, he will mail the story to the person designated on the envelope. In a few hours it will be in print and KGB will have the news."

There was a long, thumping silence in the office. MacNeal and General Brook looked at each other, at Gallagher, then back at each other again. At last MacNeal said, "You know what's at stake here, Jim. Why are you doing this?"

"I have to do it," Gallagher said, "and you know I have to do it. I'm going to kill him."

"Then we can't win either way, can we?" General Brook said.

"Maybe not," Gallagher said. "If you hold me now, the story will come out in six days and that will be the end of it. But if you let me go, at least you'll have time to maneuver. Before I can find Ramsey, you might figure out a way to stop me."

"I may know a way right now," General Brook said. "Money." He looked at Gallagher, then at MacNeal before he went on. "Your being officially dead puts you in an awkward

109

position financially. Who's going to put up the money for this manhunt of yours?"

"You are," Gallagher said.

"You think so? And why would we do that?"

Gallagher smiled, stretched out his arm in front of him and pointed his finger at the typewritten page lying in the center of MacNeal's desk.

General Brook studied the paper carefully for a long moment. Then he said, "You can't buck our whole organization, Gallagher. We'll find a way to stop you and you know it."

"I'm sure you will," Gallagher said, standing up and walking to the office door. Then, just before he opened the door and walked out, he said, "The question is—will you find it soon enough?"

part **|||**

ON A DOUBLE BED IN A PAINT-FLAKING-FROM-THE-CEILING room in a hotel in New York's West Forties, Gallagher lay reading, his head propped on a pillow. From time to time his finger tips touched his two-week-old, full but carefully trimmed mustache. From seven floors down, the midday noises came up and into the room but very little light came in around the pulled down green blinds. Only the bed lamp, lighting Gallagher's book, made a yellowish hole in the dark of the room.

A knock at the door. Gallagher sat up slowly, putting his book down and putting on a pair of steel-rimmed spectacles as he walked across the room.

Standing at the door he said, "Who is it?"

"It's your food you ordered."

Gallagher, keeping the door on the chain, opened it a few inches. Outside, a sagging older man, wearing a greenish-black, trimmed-in-orange-braid, bellhop's uniform, stood waiting, a carton of coffee in one hand, a brown paper bag in the other.

"Come in," Gallagher said. He opened the door and stood back as the man shuffled in. "Put it over there on the table by the bed. How much do I owe you?"

Putting the food on the table, the old man came back toward Gallagher, straining his eyes to read a crumpled green restaurant check he held in his hand. Gallagher switched on the ceiling light.

"That's a dollar thirty," the bellhop said. "Pastrami on rye, French fries, and a carton of coffee black."

Gallagher counted out some money into the cracked dry hand and said, "What about the clothes?"

"I went over there just a while ago," the man said. "Over to Howard Clothes right around the corner on Broadway. I talked to a fella there . . .," he took a small white card out of his jacket pocket and peered at it, ". . . a man named Farber. Alan Farber, it says here. I told him just what you wanted and he said they had it all right. Everything you said. And in your size too."

Gallagher asked him if they would deliver to the hotel and the bellhop said yes. "He said they'll deliver all right. But not till they've got the money."

"How much will it be?" Gallagher asked.

The man turned the card over and read from the back, "For the tweed suit and a felt hat and a raincoat, that's a hundred and twenty-four dollars. With tax he said it would be a hundred and thirty dollars and change."

"All right," Gallagher said. "Here's a hundred and thirty-five dollars. How soon can you go back over there and pick up the things?"

The old man said he had a few errands to do first. Running out for sandwiches and a couple of trips to the dry cleaners.

"How soon can you go then?" Gallagher asked.

"A little after three, maybe. Four o'clock at the latest. You don't want the store to deliver the stuff, huh?"

"No," Gallagher said. "I want you to pick it up. Four o'clock will be fine." He opened the door and the bellhop went out into the hallway.

He turned back suddenly, then, his eyes squinting up at Gallagher. "The tweed suit he said you'd have to take in either a gray or a green. The brown they're all sold out."

"Green's all right," Gallagher said.

"You still want the brown hat then?"

"Brown or gray. Either one."

"I told the fellow brown before. I guess I'll go ahead and get brown."

Gallagher watched the old man shuffle down the hall toward the elevator. Then he closed the door and locked it. Walking into the bathroom, he studied his mustached and bespectacled reflection in the mirror over the sink. He lifted his hand to his face, his fingertips lightly tracing the smooth scar welt on his forehead. Then, snapping off the bathroom light, he went into the other room and lay back down on the bed.

Across the street from the hotel, in a third-floor office looking out on the street, a young man with smooth black hair, wearing a brown tweed jacket, sat by the window. An eight-millimeter motion-picture camera stood on a tripod beside him, its lens focused downward through the shades at the hotel entrance. Around the young man's neck hung two cameras, a Zeiss Ikon, and a Leica with a telescopic lens attached. Binoculars to his eyes, he never turned his face away from the window, never allowed his eyes to leave the hotel entrance.

At a few minutes before five that afternoon, the heat rising stickily from the streets, perspiring, collars-open, jackets-off people jostling through the crosstown streets toward the subways, he quickly put down the binoculars, touched a switch that started the movie camera whirring, and, standing close against the shades, the Leica lens aimed at the entrance, began rapidly to click pictures.

At ten o'clock the following morning, MacNeal and Maslow sat in General Brook's office, the three of them studying, passing back and forth to each other, a sheaf of eight-by-ten photographs. They showed Gallagher leaving his hotel, pausing apparently for a moment in the entrance, then side and back views as he walked east toward Sixth Avenue.

"He's all set now," Maslow said. "He has his plane reservation and his passport. He got it from Arjac."

"Carl Kellogg, right?"

"That's right," Maslow said. "That's the name on his passport."

"How about the money?" General Brook said.

"We deposited five thousand for him at Chase Manhattan in New York. He drew it out last week. And there'll be regular deposits made for him at the Bank of England. Until we stop them," MacNeal said.

"And you say he's leaving tonight?" General Brook said.

"At 12:05," Maslow said. "TWA to London."

"Who did he see in New York?" General Brook asked.

"Only Arjac," Maslow said. "Nobody else. He saw him the day he got to New York and again yesterday when he picked up his credentials. The rest of the time he stayed in the hotel." MacNeal asked if anybody came to see him there and Maslow said, "Somebody could have slipped in but we don't think so."

"He knows he's being watched, doesn't he?"

"I'm sure he does," MacNeal said. "He's no fool. And we've had men on him twenty-four hours a day since he walked out of here. There'll be a man on the plane and a new team will pick him up when he lands in London. Beyond that, all we can do is sit tight."

"Yeah," General Brook said, "sit tight and try to find that damned piece of paper."

■ 2 ■

IT WAS A CLEAR AND UNUSUALLY SUNNY EARLY AUTUMN IN London. Gallagher took a suite of rooms at the Euston House, a modestly priced but well-kept hotel at the end of Kensington Gardens. He spent the next two or three weeks, camera-over-shoulder, benevolent and pleasant features in place, a new Scotch briar clenched between his teeth, strolling the squares and the parks and the museum floors, taking educational bus tours, prowling the Royal Academy and the Tate, attending a series of four organ concerts at Royal Albert Hall, arising early to explore the Hadenhall and Billingsgate markets, dining in a wide range of restaurants, tea shops, and pubs, amusing himself at the Drury Lane, the Haymarket, the Criterion, and the Windmill Music Hall, and generally disporting himself like a pleasantly restrained American on an extended educational and pleasure tour of London *et environs*.

Near the end of the third week, Gallagher sat in a pub down a narrow street a few doors off Cavendish Square. Sitting with him at a window table was a dark-suited, well-turned-out older man with a white mustache. And spectacles on a black ribbon.

"Of course I could spend a lot of time with road maps and so forth and work it out myself," Gallagher was saying, "but I thought it would be much wiser to get a driver. Then I'll have all my time free for research."

"That seems sensible," his companion said. "You say you've found a fellow then?"

"I think so," Gallagher said. "We've only talked on the telephone but I'm sure he'll work out fine. He's meeting me here today as a matter of fact. I told him I'd be at a table near the front windows."

"Well, you've managed that all right."

"Yes," Gallagher said, "I'm sure we'll make connections."

"And you say you plan to be here in England for about a year?"

"Yes," Gallagher said, "or a little more. My sabbatical is for just the one school year, which means I'd have to be back at the University next fall. But fortunately the head of the department is very interested in this project of mine. He's done a lot of work on Dryden himself. So I'm sure there'll be no problem if I want to stay away for another semester. If I do that I'll be back in the States a year from this coming January."

"Well," the man said, "that is a good long time."

"I'll need it," Gallagher said. "There's a lot of ground to be covered."

"I thought all you scholars kept pretty close to your books and your libraries."

"Not any more. You see the facets of Dryden and the Restoration that I'm concerned with can only be clarified by a careful examination of provincial England today. The influence of Dryden and, to a lesser degree, of Pope can only be illustrated by the present evidence. . . ."

"Excuse me," the man with the white mustache said. He nodded his head toward the door. "Do you think that might be your man?"

Gallagher turned in his chair and looked toward the front door. A husky, clean-faced man stood there, wearing a belted dark suit, and holding a cap in his hands.

"Yes," Gallagher said, "I think it might be." He got up from the table then and walked over to the man at the door.

For the next five days, Gallagher seemed simply to be continuing his tour-in-depth of London. Now, however, by private car. Riding in an English Ford driven by the man who had come to meet him in the pub off Cavendish Square. As they drove along, walked to and from the car, or sat in pubs or restaurants, they seemed always to be in conversation. Or, more accurately, the driver, it seemed, was listening while Gallagher talked. On the sixth day, Gallagher checked out of his hotel, and the two men headed south out of London.

In Washington one autumn afternoon, the sun grayed-over and cool and almost out of sight behind the trees and a cold rain falling since noon, MacNeal and General Brook and Harris came into the parking lot and got into Brook's car. Harris driving, the other two men in the back seat.

"Where did Gallagher meet this guy?" General Brook asked as they closed the rear doors and settled in, Harris starting the engine and pulling out into the exit lane.

"We don't know," MacNeal said. "Korea maybe. Or maybe he didn't know him before. Maybe somebody steered them together."

"You say his name's Castor?"

"That's right," MacNeal said. "Roy Castor. He's fifty-eight years old and he's lived in London since he retired five years ago."

"What about before then?" General Brook asked.

MacNeal said he was from a little town in the north of England. "He was a merchant seaman. Later he worked himself up to Sergeant Major in the Scotch Guards and from there he went into British Intelligence. Retired from there five years ago."

"What's he been doing since he retired?"

"Nothing. He has a small garden out near the north edge of London. He grows flowers and vegetables. He spends a lot of time out there."

"Is he married?" General Brook asked.

"He was," MacNeal said, "but his wife's been dead for a long time. He has a married daughter who lives in Copenhagen."

"Anything else?" General Brook asked.

"Just that he's a good man," MacNeal said, "and a tough one. And he knows England like his pocket."

General Brook asked him then if he had any idea where they were heading.

"They seem to be winding around a lot," MacNeal said, "but they're moving gradually south toward Portsmouth."

"And from there, they'll go to Cardiff and Bristol and the rest of the seaports," Brook said.

"That's what we expect," MacNeal said.

"They're not so dumb," General Brook said.

"They're not dumb at all," MacNeal said, looking out the window at the streetlights starting to blink on in the dark late afternoon.

■ 3 ■

IT WAS OCTOBER NOW. A LATE, RAINY NIGHT IN PORTSMOUTH.
In a saloon, crowded and loud and smoky, on the west side of
the harbor, where the cattle boats and coal boats filled up or
emptied out, Castor sat at a table with a seaman named
Bingham, a freckled Welshman with hard hands and bent legs,
and two forty-odd-year-old women. One named Lillian, a na-
tive of Portsmouth, born less than five minutes' walk from
where she now sat, and the other a bulging, homemade blonde
named Eunice who, coming originally from Glasgow, was
known to have earned as high as fifty pounds a night for the
multiple sale of her body when she was in her early twenties.
Now, however, she was much better off, she insisted, because
having neither youth nor beauty nor reputation to maintain, she
was free to swill beer and dip fried chips in tomato sauce with
anyone who asked her and in her furnished room later to fall,
naked and voracious, upon anyone she chose, with no
consideration for the amount of money it might bring her, if
any. "I was never cut out for a whore," she said. "I like men too
much."

Castor, paying for another round of drinks, was saying, "I've
had a few cushy jobs in my day, but this one is undoubtedly the
cushiest. I drive this citizen, this gentleman of learning, about
the countryside, while he carries on like an idiot about poetry
and the eighteenth century and God-knows-what-all. And
always with his nose in a book or else in the clouds. I don't
imagine he's seen a tree or a shrub or a cow in the fields since
we left London."

"He sounds dotty," Lillian said.

"Dotty's not the word for it," Castor said.

"But he pays you a good wage, don't he, Roy?" Eunice said.

"Yes, he does," Castor said, "and all expenses in addition. Like I say, it's cushy enough as far as money's concerned. Like all the rest of the Americans, he's got enough money all right."

"Sounds like an interesting fellow," Eunice said. "He doesn't sound dotty to me. I guess I'd like to meet him."

"You've got your hands full with me," Bingham said. "Never mind worrying about some bloody American schoolteacher. You've got your hands full as it is."

"It ain't her hands she's thinkin' about," Lillian said.

"If you say it's you that I've got my hands full of," Eunice said to Bingham, "you have a high opinion of yourself. I can polish off four like you between breakfast and my bath."

"To tell the truth," Castor said, "I don't think you'd want this American, Eunice. He'd probably want to flatten you out with a steam-iron and use you for a bookmark."

Next morning, driving west from Portsmouth, the rain falling harder now than it had last night, Castor said, "I gave them a bit of a show as you and I agreed I should and they took it all in like cow's cream. I'm afraid I made you sound like something of a jackass. Hope you don't mind."

"I don't mind," Gallagher said.

"I also got in a couple of licks at Americans generally. That might come in handy later on."

"Were the same two guys there?" Gallagher asked then.

"One the same," Castor said. "One new one. Either somebody's tailing the man who's tailing us or we're being watched from two different directions."

Gallagher looked out at the rain. "It's a lousy day," he said then.

"We do it to discourage tourists," Castor said.

"I have a hunch we're going to have a long search, Roy."

"Maybe so, maybe not," Castor said, "but long or not, we'll find your friend, Mr. Ramsey. Don't worry about that."

All through October and November and well into December they drove along the southern, then up the western perimeter of England. Stopping, starting, staying in one spot for a week, another for two days. In and out of water-front hotels and restaurants and saloons and whorehouses. Watching and listening and waiting. Trying to learn without asking. Never asking or attracting attention. Fading in and out of Portsmouth, Dover, Southampton, Bournemouth and looping back and coming in again. Listening and being present where the seamen were. Castor doing most of the listening. Blending in with the seamen and the dock workers and the barmaids and the whores. And waiting. And listening hard while he watched for a man or some sign of a man like Ramsey. Weymouth and Torquay and the little coastal towns and fishing villages along the way, between and on either side. Plymouth and Devonport and Falmouth and St. Ives. Then back to London. Another week around the harbors there. Taking the train to London. Then back to Plymouth to pick up the car again. After the fruitless London week was over.

Up the western edge then, the sea edge, and in around the loop and up to Bristol and Cardiff. Newport and Port Talbot and Swansea. It was raining a lot now and the days were short and even before the dark came down in the evening, it was dark from the ocean fog and the rain and the coming-on of winter. On out to Pembroke and around and heading north again along Cardigan Bay. Stopping at the small ports and harbors too. Sometimes for only a few hours. New Quay and Barnmouth and Harlech, Nevin and Bangor. On east then through Colwyn Bay to Liverpool. Up to Southport and back again to Liverpool. A long stay there, with Castor unshaved and profligate, night and day in the water-front saloons and the wind getting colder and more raw each morning, blowing in from the west across the Irish Sea.

MacNeal and Harris and Maslow sat in General Brook's office. A heavy wet snow was falling outside the window, muffling all the sounds from the street and the parking lot down below.

"It's getting late, boys," General Brook said. "I don't have to tell you that it's getting very damned late. The first thing you know it's going to be Christmas and we're still dragging our asses around Washington trying to find the twin brother to this." He held up a folded sheet of paper.

MacNeal said, "I think we'll have to spread out more."

"Like where?" General Brook said.

"California," MacNeal said. "Gallagher went to school out there. He has a lot of old friends there. One of them might give us the answer."

"We sent two men to California a month ago. They didn't come up with anything," General Brook said.

"I know they didn't," MacNeal said. "But we'll just have to try again. We'll have to dig deeper, that's all."

"All right, Harry," General Brook said. "Go ahead. But if we don't come up with something soon, we're really going to have our tails in a crack." His intercom buzzed. "Yes? Yes, I see. Thank you." He turned back to MacNeal and said, "Well, that's some good news anyway. Our people picked up Ramsey's trail again. He's back in England."

"Where is he now?" MacNeal asked.

"They've planted him in a cover job. With the International Maritime Welfare Board. They say he'll get around a lot but his headquarters seem to be in Newcastle."

"Well at least we know where he is," MacNeal said.

"Yeah," General Brook said, "but if we can find him, so can Gallagher."

▪ 4 ▪

CASTOR AND GALLAGHER, TOGETHER DAY AFTER DAY AS THE rain rolled down the windshield in front of them or fell outside their hotel windows, talked a lot. More accurately, Gallagher, after having exhausted all memories, incidents, and descriptions which featured or in any way clarified Ramsey, sat back and listened while Castor talked. He talked about his parents, both dead now and buried in Brecknock, a village in Wales where they had grown up, married and spent their entire lives together. He talked of his older brother, Simon, a retired clergyman and a widower like Roy, now living in Birmingham with their younger sister, Agnes, her second husband, John Blaine, and her two sons by her first marriage, that husband having been killed in North Africa under Montgomery. And mostly, driving along the walled country roads and straining his eyes to see the way ahead through the rain, he talked about his wife.

"She was never a big, sturdy woman. But she was tough.

When she was in a family way with the baby, she went about her regular work in the house and didn't complain or expect extra attention the way so many women do. If I tried to get her to stay in bed a bit late of a morning she'd get about half mad at me. 'If I look like an invalid, then you'd best find yourself another woman,' she'd say to me. And when I'd finished shaving off my whiskers and gone downstairs, there she'd be. Coffee steaming and the oatmeal in the bowl waiting for the warm cream to be poured on it. My daughter is big and strong, more like my people, but she doesn't have what her mother had. A sweet girl and pretty as a face in a magazine. Always been a good daughter, too, with no problems or carrying on. But she doesn't have the steel in her spine that her mother did."

Gallagher never spoke about Joannie. The image of her sitting in the front seat of the car, that early gray morning in Santa Monica with Ellen in her arms and tears rolling down her cheeks, was locked into position behind his eyes and in his throat and it would not allow him to speak.

In California, Maslow and Harris and Woodson were in day-and-night motion trying to untangle a knotted skein of old friendships and associations which might perhaps uncover one person who by a word or facial expression would reveal that he or she knew that Gallagher was still alive. That person might be the one he had entrusted with the letter.

"Gallagher is to be given a posthumous award by the State Department. Along with the medallion, a bound volume of biographical material will be included. We are looking for information to be used in this biography. Anything at all you can tell us will be greatly appreciated."

Over and over, they made, each of them, this little set speech. In Los Angeles, Pasadena, Berkeley, San Francisco. All up and down the coast where the classmates, friends and Korean veterans who knew Gallagher had settled. They made the speech, then sat back to listen. And wait. And in Washington, General Brook waited.

One early morning in the second week of December, Castor came out the side door of a country inn thirty kilometers west of London. Gallagher followed close behind him. They put their luggage in the trunk of the car and got into the front seat. As Castor started the engine and began to back out of the parking space, a hotel porter came out the side entrance. "Just a moment, sir." He walked over to the car, holding an envelope in his hand.

"What is it?" Castor said as the porter came up to the car.

"A messenger was here very early this morning. Left this envelope for you."

"For me or Mr. Kellogg?" Castor said.

"I didn't take it myself," the porter said, "but I believe the night man said it was for Mr. Kellogg."

"Thank you," Castor said and the porter turned and walked back toward the doorway. The two men looked at the envelope Castor held in his hand.

"It's from Ramsey," Gallagher said.

"Ramsey? How do you know?"

"I don't know," Gallagher said, "but I've got a strong hunch. Open it and see." Castor tore off one end of the envelope, shook it, and a white card slid out. He turned it over and read it. "Am I right?" Gallagher said.

"You're right," Castor said. "It says, 'I hope you're enjoying your tour of England.' And it's signed, 'Brian.'" He handed the card to Gallagher. "Is that his handwriting?"

"Yes," Gallagher said.

"What do you make of it?" Castor asked.

"It's very simple," Gallagher said. "He knows I'm alive and looking for him. And he wants me to know he knows it."

"Why would he do that?" Castor said.

"The idea probably amuses him," Gallagher said. "Brian has a great sense of humor."

"What do we do now?" Castor said.

"We keep looking," Gallagher said.

That night before he went to bed, Gallagher shaved off his mustache and packed the steel-rimmed spectacles away in his luggage.

■ 5 ■

GENERAL BROOK STOOD LOOKING OUT MACNEAL'S OFFICE WIN-
dow at early evening Washington. It had been a gray, slushy
day and the beginning darkness now was heavy and muddy. As
he watched, the Christmas lights were twinkling and
flickering on all over the city and a huge Christmas tree burned
blue and yellow on Pennsylvania Avenue.

"Harris is still out there. Right?" MacNeal said to Maslow
who was sitting across the desk from him.

"He's in Berkeley," Maslow said. "That's where we wound
up."

General Brook turned from the window now. "And you've
got nothing at all to go on?"

"Not a ripple," Maslow said.

"That's a hell of a note," General Brook said.

"Is Harris still digging?" MacNeal asked.

"No," Maslow said. "We exhausted every lead we had. He's
just waiting for a call from me. Either giving him new instructions or ordering him back here."

"Well, let's get him back," General Brook said. "No point in
his sitting on his can out there. We'll have to come up with
something else." Then, "Any ideas, Harry?"

"Nothing great," MacNeal said, "but there is something
that's been going around in my head the last few days."

"What's that?" General Brook said.

"Well," MacNeal said, "we've got nowhere by checking
Gallagher's friends and we can't seem to get anything out of the
newspaper people without making them suspicious. So let's try

125

another tack. Let's assume that Jim approached this whole thing in a completely businesslike way. Let's assume that he dealt with a stranger rather than somebody he knew before."

"If he did that, we're really up a creek," General Brook said.

"Maybe not," MacNeal said. "Who would you go to if you had some complicated business to transact and you needed help from somebody you could trust?"

"I guess I'd go to a lawyer," General Brook said.

"That's right. So would I," MacNeal said. "So why wouldn't Gallagher do the same thing?"

Maslow said, "That makes sense to me."

"What do you think?" MacNeal said to Brook.

"I don't know," General Brook said, "it sounds too simple. But on the other hand. . . ."

"We can move fast with lawyers," Maslow said. "We can lay it on the line with them and get some quick answers. If they know anything."

"It won't be like pussy-footing around with Jim's friends," MacNeal said. "We can move quickly. So even if it turns out to be a blind alley, we won't have wasted much time."

"How much time?" General Brook said.

"With ten men," Maslow said, "I'd say from ten days to two weeks."

General Brook walked to the window again and looked out at the lights. A new snow had started to fall. He turned back after a moment and said, "All right. Let's do it."

In a dingy hotel near the wharves in Plymouth, Gallagher and Castor sat sprawled in two ancient upholstered chairs, the remains of a meal on a table shoved to one side. Outside in the wet streets carolers were singing and church chimes far uptown away from the docks were playing a Christmas song. Gallagher leaned forward, picked up a half-empty brandy bottle from the floor and refilled Castor's glass.

"Merry Christmas," he said.

"Merry Christmas," Castor said as Gallagher filled his own glass.

"What do you think, Roy?" Gallagher asked then, settling back in his chair.

"I don't know," Castor said.

"I think we're nailed to the floor," Gallagher said.

Castor said he wasn't as optimistic as he had been earlier in the fall.

"I'm not optimistic at all," Gallagher said. "I think we're nailed."

"It's a big country to hide in," Castor said, "but I thought we'd have some luck by now. It's over three months and we've had no luck at all. I was expecting some kind of luck within two months at the outside."

"Instead of us following Ramsey," Gallagher said, "he's got a tail on us. A whole platoon of them, judging by the number of faces we keep seeing."

"Do you think he'll take another crack at you?" Castor asked.

"I don't know," Gallagher said, "but he's not playing cat-and-mouse for nothing."

"Your people in Washington must know where he is."

"You bet they do," Gallagher said.

"And they know where we are," Castor said.

"No doubt about that," Gallagher said.

"But I have a hunch," Castor said, "they don't know Ramsey's tailing us."

"I have a hunch you're right," Gallagher said.

"What if you told MacNeal or General Brook that Ramsey already knows you're alive? Wouldn't that take the pressure off you?"

"Maybe," Gallagher said.

"Maybe you ought to tell them," Castor said.

"Maybe I should," Gallagher said, "but I'm not going to. I don't want to take a chance that the whole thing will blow up and Ramsey will be pulled out of England."

"Do you think KGB knows you're still alive?" Castor said.

"No, I don't," Gallagher said. "If they knew, something would happen. Either to me or to Ramsey. They're still fooled, I think."

"If you're right," Castor said, "then Ramsey is playing a dangerous game."

"That's the way he likes to play," Gallagher said.

The phone rang then and Castor got up to answer it.

"Yes. No. Yes, he's here. Just a moment. It's for you," he said, holding the receiver out to Jim. "Long distance." As Gallagher took the phone, Castor quickly went to the hall door, opened it, and went outside the room.

"Hello," Jim said. "Yes, operator, this is Mr. Kellogg."

A muffled voice said then, "Merry Christmas, Jimbo."

"Who is this?" Gallagher said.

"It's me, Brian," the voice said. "I just wanted to say Merry

Christmas and tell you I sent you a gift. You'll find it in the glove compartment of your car. And you don't have to worry about opening it. It's not a bomb." There was a click then and the line went dead.

"Hello," Jim said. "Hello. . . ."

The operator came on then and said, "I'm sorry, sir, but your party has left the wire."

"Yes, all right. Thank you." As he hung up the receiver, Castor came back into the room.

"I just popped down into the switchboard room," Castor said. "That call came from Newcastle."

Two hours later, MacNeal, in a dinner jacket, left his cocktail guests and went into the library to pick up the phone.

"Yes, Walter," he said.

"I just had a code call from England," General Brook said, "and I don't like the sound of it."

"What's up?" MacNeal said.

"Gallagher's on a plane heading for Newcastle. He'll be there in about an hour and a half."

"Is he warm?" MacNeal asked.

"We don't know," General Brook said. "But we can't take any chances. Our people alerted the Newcastle police and they've already picked up a couple of Ramsey's friends. That should get Ramsey on the run. We expect him to be out of town within an hour."

Inside a medium-sized plane flying north toward Newcastle, Gallagher and Castor sat well up front away from the dozen or so other passengers scattered through the cabin. They talked quietly.

"I lived there for nearly three years," Castor said. "I know Newcastle like I know my own clothes closet."

"Where do we start?" Gallagher said.

"Same as usual. The water front. There's an old seamen's hotel called the Stafford House. It's about three blocks from the wharves. We'll check in there. Right across the street is a pub called the Victoria. Every sailor who hits Newcastle ends up there sooner or later. And Sarah Spender knows them all."

"Who's she?" Gallagher asked.

"An old lady friend of mine," Castor said. "Actually she's not all that old and she's not such a lady either but she is a good friend still. She runs the Victoria and there's nothing going on in Newcastle that she doesn't know about. If Ramsey has an eye for the ladies, as you say, then he must have given Sarah a pinch now and again. If so, she'll remember him. She never forgets a pinch."

■ 6 ■

SARAH SPENDER, STOUT, ATTRACTIVE, AND IN HER LATE FOR-ties, stood firmly behind the bar of the Victoria. A famous local beauty in her girlhood and young womanhood, she was lovely still, erect and firm-fleshed with a high color to her cheeks, clear blue eyes, and strong teeth in a laughing, full-lipped mouth. Her arms were bare and round and dimpled at the elbows. There was a delicate scent of talcum powder about her and her breasts pushed softly together and swelled smoothly above the line of her low-cut dress. "A gentleman comes in here, he deserves a good, honest drink and something pretty to look at while he drinks it."

Across the heads of the men and a few women who sat or stood in the big room, fireplace at one end, she saw through the front window, through the tinsel and banners and strung pop-corn garlands hanging there, a car pull up and stop at the curb outside. A moment later, two middle-sized men, one in a heavy overcoat, the other in a tweed suit with a knitted sweater under the jacket, both wearing soft hats, came through the door-way and pushed their way through the crowd and up to the bar. They ordered stout and stood at the rail sipping it, their backs to Sarah, their eyes glancing about the room. They fin-ished their stout and the man in the tweed suit had another one, while the man in the overcoat lighted a cigarette and continued to inspect the people in the room. At last, the two men walked over to a large round table by the window. One of them bent over to speak to a black-haired man who sat there with two other men and a ginger-haired girl. When the two men walked back out through the door, got into their car and drove away, the black-haired man went with them. As the car pulled away outside, one of the two men left at the table with the girl got

129

up deliberately, walked to a pay telephone in the corner by the washroom entrance, closed himself behind the glass door, and began to dial a number.

At the Newcastle airport, Gallagher and Castor came out of the terminal building and got into a maroon and blue taxicab. "Stafford House," Castor said, "and we're in a hurry."

In an apartment in a quiet residential neighborhood, about a mile from the Victoria, a telephone rang sharply in a dark room. Five times. A door opened and Ramsey came out of the lighted bedroom, wearing pajamas and carrying a drink. He walked to the phone and picked it up. "Yes," he said. He listened for a moment. Then—"Yes, I see. Thank you." He hung up the phone and walked easily back into the bedroom. A young Negro girl with very short hair and wearing a man's pajama top sat in a deep leather chair, her legs stretched out in front of her, her feet, ankles crossed, resting on the foot of the bed.

"Could I interest you in a holiday in the country?" Ramsey said, stepping out of his pajama pants and walking to the closet.

"Yes, you could," the girl said.

"Can you leave in five minutes?" he said, pulling on a pair of underwear shorts.

"Yes," the girl said, standing up and pulling the pajama top off over her head.

"Then we'll leave in five minutes," Ramsey said.

In a second-floor room of the Stafford House, Gallagher stood at the window, looking down into the street at the entrance of the Victoria. As he watched from behind the shade, Castor came out of the entrance, stood at the curb a moment, then walked across the street and disappeared through the hotel entrance. Still watching the Victoria, Gallagher saw a thin man in a soft tweed hat step out through the doorway. He stood at the curb, looking after Castor, and lighted a cigarette.

A few minutes later, still at the window, Gallagher listened carefully to Castor who sat on the edge of the bed smoking as he talked.

"She says the police picked up a couple of men a few hours ago and then a while ago they dropped in and picked up another one. It's pretty quiet over there now."

"And she doesn't know anything about Ramsey?" Gallagher said.

"The name, Ramsey, doesn't mean anything to her," Castor said. "She said she'd have to see a picture of him."

Gallagher said he had some snapshots of Ramsey in his luggage. "You can show one of those to her." Then, "Can you trust her to keep her mouth shut?"

"I can't guarantee it," Castor said, "but she's a reasonably good risk."

"We don't have much choice," Gallagher said, "so I guess we'll have to trust her." He looked out the window again. "I have a sneaking suspicion our rabbit jumped out of the trap."

"It smells that way," Castor said.

"And I have a hunch," Gallagher said, "that my old friends in Washington held the trap door open."

"What now?" Castor said.

"We'll wait," Gallagher said. "You talk to your girl friend again tomorrow and show her the picture. Then we'll see where we go from there. There's no use chasing around till we have somebody to chase."

In Washington, Maslow walked into a large and imposing office building, the third such building he'd canvassed that day, the twenty-second in the last nine days. He checked the building directory, looked at a small notebook he carried in his pocket, then got into the elevator. An hour later, when he came down in the elevator and left the building, a man was with him. An older man. A well-dressed older man named Compton. Maslow walked briskly now, his briefcase held tightly under one arm.

Next afternoon, Castor sat in the back room of the Victoria in a booth with Sarah. She held a snapshot in her hand, a picture of Ramsey leaning against the fender of an open sports car, smiling.

"It's the same man, all right," Sarah said finally. "He has a beard now and he walks with a limp. But it's the same man. Joseph Norman, he calls himself now. He's generous with his friends. Buys them drinks more often than not. It's him all right."

Back in the hotel room, Castor repeated the entire conversation to Gallagher. "He's just as much a ladies' man as ever," he said. "He's been after Sarah, she says, ever since he came here."

131

"That might help us out, if and when he comes back here," Gallagher said. "Does she have any idea where he is?"

"Out of town, she says, since sometime yesterday. She's not sure where he ran to, but a couple of his friends were talking this morning, she said, about Bristol."

In MacNeal's office in Washington, Mr. Compton shook hands with General Brook and MacNeal, then turned and followed Maslow out into the hall. Behind him, in the office, General Brook picked up a piece of folded paper, unfolded it, and smoothed it out on the desktop. "We're in business now, Harry," he said. "Let's pick him up."

In a small prop-jet flying from Newcastle to Birmingham to Bristol, Castor turned to Gallagher and said, "I have a feeling we're getting warm."

"So do I," Gallagher said.

"You think he still has a tail on us?"

"I wouldn't be surprised," Gallagher said. "I saw our skinny friend with the tweed hat at the airport in Newcastle."

"I can't figure out why Ramsey doesn't make a move," Castor said.

"He will," Gallagher said, "but not till he's ready. I have a hunch he feels safe. We didn't fool him but we fooled the KGB. So he can take his time."

"But what's he have to gain by this cat-and-mouse game?"

"Like I told you before," Gallagher said, "it probably amuses him."

■ 7 ■

A MAN CARRYING A LIGHT-COLORED RAINCOAT OVER HIS ARM walked out the main exit of the Bristol air terminal. He stopped at the the curb where a string of taxis and private cars were waiting. Taking the raincoat off his arm he shook it out and slowly put it on. He buttoned it up tightly around his neck and turned the collar up. In a black limousine parked thirty feet away, a uniformed driver turned his head slightly toward the back seat and said, "That's our man."

Gallagher and Castor came out of the terminal then and walked straight to a waiting taxi. As they pulled away from the curb, the man in the light raincoat walked briskly to the limousine and got into the back seat. The black car pulled out and followed behind the taxi. Another black car pulled out then and followed the limousine. The thin man in the tweed hat stood in the doorway and watched the three cars pull away from the terminal area. Then he turned and walked back into the building.

A few minutes later, their taxi approaching the outskirts of Bristol, rolling swiftly past the aircraft plants, the sugar refineries, breweries, chemical plants, and warehouses, Gallagher glanced over his shoulder at the two cars hard on the tail of the taxicab. He turned his eyes forward again and said to Castor, "I have a feeling we're not alone."

"I have the same feeling," Castor said. "What do you suggest?"

"We don't seem to have much choice," Gallagher said. "Let's relax and see what happens."

It happened quickly. The third car in line pulled past the limousine and the taxi, cut in ahead of the taxi sharply and began immediately to slow down. Boxed in from the front and with the limousine in back riding his bumper, then sliding up beside him so he couldn't swerve to the next lane, the cab driver slowed down at the same rate as the preceding car and at last pulled off to the side of the road, the other two cars still boxing him in, front and side. Three men got out of the front car and two men out of the limousine. They ranged themselves on either side of the taxi as Castor and Gallagher deliberately climbed out.

Half an hour later, in a house just behind St. Mark's Chapel, Harris turned away from a second-story window and said, "Here they come. The cars just pulled into the drive."

Harry MacNeal, sitting comfortably on a sofa, several file folders of papers beside him and a fire crackling in the fireplace to his right, said then, "Send Gallagher in by himself. I want to see him alone."

A few minutes later, Gallagher sat in an easy chair, soft and cretonne-covered, facing MacNeal. Legs crossed, hands loosely folded in his lap.

133

"So you're taking me back to the States?" Gallagher said. "Is that it?"

"That's it, Jim," MacNeal said. "We have to do it."

"What if I don't want to go?" Gallagher said.

MacNeal said he knew he didn't want to go but they had to take him anyway.

"I see," Gallagher said. Then, "Harry, what if I told you that Ramsey knows I'm alive?"

"I'd say that's all the more reason to get you out of here."

"If he knows," Gallagher said, "don't you think KGB knows, too?"

"What makes you think Ramsey knows?" MacNeal said.

"I talked with him on the telephone."

"I can't swallow that one, Jim," MacNeal said.

"Swallow it or not, it's true," Gallagher said. "He called me."

"What did he say?"

"He wished me a Merry Christmas."

"Sure he did," MacNeal said.

"And he sent me a gift," Gallagher went on. "He sent me a pocket compass. I've got it right here." He pulled a small compass out of his jacket pocket and handed it to MacNeal. Out of his billfold, he took a small white card. "And here's the card he enclosed. Read it."

MacNeal took the card, looked at it, read aloud, "Here's a little equipment to help you in your search. Merry Christmas, Brian."

"What do you think of that?" Gallagher said.

"Nice try, Jim. But I don't buy it."

Gallagher said it was Ramsey's handwriting on the card.

"Maybe it is and maybe it isn't," MacNeal said, "but before I have a chance to find out for sure, you're going to be in Washington."

Gallagher reached over and took the compass and the card from MacNeal. He put them back into his pocket. Then he said, "I don't think so, Harry."

"Even if Ramsey does know you're alive," MacNeal said, "it wouldn't change our position. We know there's been another tail on you and maybe Ramsey put it there. But whether he knows about you or not, KGB doesn't know and that's the important thing."

"Are you sure they don't know?" Gallagher said.

"If they did," MacNeal said, "Ramsey wouldn't be operating. They'd have him out of England before you could snap your fingers. No, Jim, he's doing an important job for them. There's been more work stoppage and labor unrest around the seaports in the past four months than there had been in a year and a half before he showed up. He's doing his job all right."

"But you're saying that wouldn't matter if KGB found out about me?"

"That's right," MacNeal said. "They wouldn't trust him and they'd shut him off like a faucet."

"Then you're still hoping to turn him around," Gallagher said.

"You bet we are. He's in a stronger position every day. He should be a gold mine of information."

"So you're going to take me back to Washington where I can't make waves, is that it?"

"I'm afraid so, Jim," MacNeal said. "We have no choice."

Gallagher stood up and walked over to the mantel. He turned then and stood with his back to the fire.

"Well, Harry," he said, "I hate to spoil your plans but I'm afraid I've still got you buffaloed."

"What do you mean?" MacNeal said.

"That paper you got from Compton—do you have it with you?"

"No," MacNeal said. "It's in a safe in General Brook's office."

"But you read it, didn't you?" Gallagher asked.

"Of course. I read it and Walter read it and then we locked it up."

"You compared it with the first paper, didn't you? The one I left with General Brook."

"That's right. It was an exact carbon copy," MacNeal said.

"Right," Gallagher said. Then, "But the first paper was a carbon copy too, wasn't it?"

MacNeal said he didn't remember and Gallagher said, "Think hard. It was on onionskin paper. It was a carbon copy. Just like the one you got from Compton."

"What are you getting at?" MacNeal said.

"It's very simple," Gallagher said. "If there are two carbons, there must be a typewritten original someplace. Did you ever wonder where that original is?"

MacNeal got up now and walked to the window. "You're bluffing, Jim," he said.

"No, I'm not and you know I'm not."

MacNeal turned and walked back toward the fireplace.

"General Brook will never sit still for it," he said. "You can't horse him twice."

"Yes, I can," Gallagher said. "Do you think I'd be dumb enough to put all my eggs in one basket?"

"No, I guess you wouldn't," MacNeal said slowly.

"I gave one copy to Compton," Gallagher said. "You tracked that one down. The other copy, the original, is in a bank deposit box and a vice-president of the bank has the key. His instructions are the same as Compton's were. If a week goes past and he doesn't hear from me, the paper comes out of the box and he mails it to where I've addressed it." Gallagher walked back to his chair and sat down. "You're nailed, Harry, and you know it."

MacNeal stood looking at him for a long moment. Then he walked over and picked up the phone. "Tell Harris to come in," he said into the phone, "and get me a courier. I want him to leave for Washington in five minutes."

■ 8 ■

Maslow, wearing his overcoat, his hat in his hand, stood waiting in the foyer of General Brook's home. The General, in pajamas and a robe, came out of a doorway down the hall and walked over to him.

"You held the courier, didn't you?" he said.

"Yes sir," Maslow said. "He's right outside in the car and there's a jet waiting for him at the airport. He'll be back in Bristol in a few hours."

"Good," General Brook said. "The quicker, the better. Now—take down this message for MacNeal." Maslow took out a small pad and began to write. "Release Gallagher," General Brook went on, "but keep him under tight surveillance. Find some way to throw a scare into Ramsey. Keep him in the bushes till we can deal with Gallagher."

The clock in the Bristol railroad station said eight-twenty.

Gallagher walked in through the main entrance. He stood just inside, feeling the waves of heat from the overhead blowers and the cold currents of air around his ankles when an outside door opened. He walked to a newsstand then and bought a paper. As he opened it his eyes took in the station. The man with the light raincoat had sat down on a bench far off in the corner. He smoked meticulously and occupied himself with a spread-out timetable. As Gallagher's eyes came back to the door, the thin man in the tweed hat came into the station. He walked directly to the washroom. When he came out a few minutes later he went to a coffee bar against the far wall and sat there hunched over a mug of chocolate, his back to Gallagher.

Outside the station, in the parking area, a hard-looking kid of nineteen or twenty wheeled in on a badly used motorcycle. The kid, striped mufflered and leather-jacketed, clumped up the steps and into the station, pushing his hair back from his eyes with one hand. He stood just inside the door and looked around. As his eyes came to Gallagher, Jim stood up, folded his newspaper into a neat square, and walked to a wire trash container. The man in the light raincoat and the man in the tweed hat watched him from where they sat. Gallagher dropped his newspaper in the basket, turned away and found a new seat on a bench nearby.

The kid walked to the newsstand now, leafed through several magazines and bought at last a copy of *Paris Match* with Simone Signoret on the cover. Tucking it under his arm, he started for the door to the parking area.

Gallagher, a cigarette in his mouth and his fingers moving in and out of his pocket feeling for matches, stood up as the kid passed in front of him.

"Excuse me," he said, "do you have a light?"

"I think so," the kid said, reaching into a jacket pocket. "Yes. Here we are." He handed over a half-empty folder of matches.

"Thank you," Gallagher said.

"You can keep 'em if you like," the kid said, starting to move off. "I've got a lighter."

"Thanks a lot," Gallagher said. He lighted a cigarette and stood watching the kid as he moved across the station floor and out the door. Then he walked back to the bench where he had first sat.

He glanced at the raincoated man, and at the tweed-hatted man at the counter. As their eyes turned away, he looked down at the message written in ink inside the match folder. It said,

137

"The bird flew. See you at nine." Gallagher glanced at the station clock. Eight-twenty-eight. Then he lighted all the matches in the folder and watched them burn to a black ash in the ashtray set in the arm of the bench.

At nine o'clock the man in the tweed hat, on his second cup of chocolate, saw Castor come into the station and walk over to where Gallagher was sitting. Gallagher stood up and they talked together for only a moment. Then Castor walked all the way across the station floor, past the man in the tweed hat and past the man in the light raincoat and closed himself inside a telephone booth. The man in the tweed hat left the counter and walked to a bench halfway between the phone booth and Gallagher. A few minutes later when Castor came back across the floor and sat down beside Gallagher, the man in the tweed hat strolled back to the counter.

"I talked to Sarah," Castor said.

"What goes?"

"Nothing. There's no sign of Ramsey."

"No word at all?" Gallagher asked.

"Nothing," Castor said. "But a man named Luther, one of Ramsey's friends, came in while we were talking. Sarah said I should call her back at ten o'clock."

In the Bristol apartment where he had talked with Gallagher, MacNeal stood talking on the phone, Harris standing just behind him.

"Good. Stay with him," MacNeal said. "I'll be up there as soon as I can make it." He hung up and turned to Harris. "Ramsey landed at the Liverpool airport ten minutes ago."

"Now what?" Harris said.

"We'd better get up there," MacNeal said. "Just in case he decides to stop running we'll have to find a way to nudge him. General Brook wants him out of the way till we can pull Gallagher's claws."

"What if Ramsey won't run?"

"He's been running since he left Newcastle," MacNeal said.

"But he might decide to stop," Harris said. "You said so yourself."

"In that case, we have to make sure he doesn't get hurt."

"You mean we'd protect him from Gallagher?" Harris said.

MacNeal was putting on his coat. He didn't answer for a long moment. Then he said, "If we have to, yes."

"That's a switch," Harris said.

"It's a switch all right," MacNeal said. Then, "What's the latest on Gallagher?"

"He's still at the railroad station. Castor's with him."

"What are they doing?" MacNeal asked.

"They're just sitting there."

"That doesn't sound right to me," MacNeal said. "I'd like it better if they were doing something."

Harris said he didn't think they'd be sitting there like that if they had any idea where to go.

"Maybe you're right," MacNeal said, "but I still don't like the sound of it. How soon can we get a commercial flight to Liverpool?"

Harris took a small packet of timetables out of his side jacket pocket and thumbed through them quickly. "Ten-thirty," he said then.

"All right," MacNeal said, "let's get going. I'll make some calls from the airport."

At a few seconds past ten Castor in the station booth and Sarah in her office at the back of the Victoria with the door closed were talking on the telephone.

"He's in Liverpool now," Sarah said, "but I understand they expect him back in Newcastle sometime late tonight."

"Do you think he'll come to your place?"

"He usually does," she said.

"All right, Sarah," Castor said. "And you know what to do then, if he does come?"

"Don't worry, Roy," Sarah said. "I'll do my best."

"We'll be along then, love. Be careful and I'll see you later."

As Castor came out of the phone booth and walked toward him, Gallagher glanced at the station clock. Four minutes past ten. He stood up as Castor came up to the bench.

"Newcastle," Castor said.

"Newcastle? Are you sure?"

"He's in Liverpool now," Castor said, "but Sarah says he'll be in Newcastle tonight."

"Then we'll be there," Gallagher said.

"I'm not sure about the planes," Castor said. "It may be difficult getting there tonight."

"We'll get there," Gallagher said. "But before we leave here we're going to shake these two idiots. I'm getting goddamned tired of all those extra eyes watching me."

"Me too," Castor said. "What do you suggest?"

"I suggest we go in the men's room and take a long time to wash our hands."

"And then what?"

"If we're out of sight for five minutes, they'll get jumpy," Gallagher said.

"And curious," Castor said. They started walking across the station, toward the men's rest room.

■ 9 ■

IT WAS RAINING AND THE WIND HAD COME UP COLD AND CUTting when Gallagher and Castor got out of their taxi and ran into the Bristol air terminal. A jet had just taken off and was whining over their heads as they came up to the ticket counter.

"That's not the Newcastle plane, is it?" Gallagher said.

"No sir, that's our nonstop service to Liverpool. The flight to Newcastle is boarding now. It will leave in twelve minutes."

Still climbing steeply but straightening out slowly into its due north flight pattern, the Liverpool plane knifed upward through the wet darkness. MacNeal and Harris sat up forward, their legs stretched out, feet touching the bulkhead.

The public address speaker tapped and whirred a couple of times. Then the captain's voice came on, heavy with a northcountry accent. "Ladies and gentlemen, we ask you to keep your seat belts fastened if you will, please. It seems that we're in for a bit of sticky weather between here and Liverpool. We may bounce around for a few moments but there'll be nothing serious to fret about. We expect to land promptly on schedule at Liverpool. Thank you."

On the highway running northeast from Liverpool to Newcastle, a black Daimler slithered and screeched and sped through the rain. A hard-faced, weatherbeaten man with gray curly hair was driving. In the back seat a girl lay asleep, covered with a red blanket. Beside the driver sat Ramsey, eyes on the road ahead, smoking a cigarette, saying nothing.

The flight for Newcastle took off from Bristol and climbed through the rain.

"No more flights out of here tonight," Castor said. "They closed down the airport."

"How's the weather in Newcastle? Did you ask?"

"There's supposed to be weather coming east from the Irish Sea, but the man at the desk says Newcastle looks clear," Castor said.

"Keep your fingers crossed," Gallagher said.

Over an hour later, as MacNeal's plane circled for a landing at Liverpool, Ramsey's car pulled up in front of his house in Newcastle. The hood of the car gleamed black and wet under the streetlights but there was no rain falling now in Newcastle. Cold and a raw wind from the west, but no rain.

"Take Shirley inside and put her to bed," Ramsey said to the driver. "I'll take the car down to the Victoria. If I have a call from London, tell them where I am."

"What about Luther?" the driver asked.

"He'll be down there with me."

As MacNeal and Harris came into the Liverpool terminal, their clothes soaked from the short run from the plane, the terminal announcer was saying, "Passengers holding reservations for connecting flights to other points please check with your flight counters at once. Because of weather this airport is closed down until further notice. . . ."

"We picked a beautiful night," MacNeal said as they walked to the baggage claim area.

"At least we got here," Harris said. "The baggage for our flight will be over there, I think."

"Passenger MacNeal, arriving from Bristol—" a woman's voice said on the public address system, "please check the information counter. Passenger MacNeal, arriving from Bristol. . . ."

MacNeal looked at Harris, then walked toward the information desk in the center of the building.

"I'm MacNeal," he said, handing the girl his canceled ticket.

"I have a telegram for you, sir," she said, leafing quickly

141

through a sheaf of notes and wires. "Here it is. Sign right here, please."

MacNeal and Harris walked away from the counter as Mac-Neal took out the telegram and read it.

"Bad news," MacNeal said. "It's from Bristol. They lost Castor and Gallagher."

He handed the wire to Harris who read it quietly aloud, " 'Lost birds. Signs indicate they are flying to Newcastle.' What do you think that means?"

"It could mean that Gallagher knows something we don't. Either Ramsey never came to Liverpool. . . ."

"He had to," Harris said. "Our men saw him get on the plane in Bristol."

"Then," MacNeal said, "he must have headed straight for Newcastle as soon as he got here."

"Where does that put us?" Harris asked.

"In a bad spot, I'm afraid," MacNeal said. Then, "Look, I'm going to the terminal director's office and try to get a call through to General Brook. You get hold of a car and driver. And be sure you get a man who knows the roads. It's going to be a fast trip."

As Ramsey walked into the Victoria, Luther got up from a table in the corner and walked to meet him. They stood by themselves at the end of the bar and talked quietly.

"You travel quite a lot these days, don't you?" Luther said.

"Quite a lot," Ramsey said.

"I think you'd better travel a bit more. For some reason, the local police have been asking about you."

"I know," Ramsey said. "In Bristol, too. And in Liverpool."

"What's it all about?" Luther said.

"Nothing. Someone's put them up to it," Ramsey said. "They want me to run and hide.":

"This is not a very good place to hide," Luther said.

Ramsey smiled and put his hand on Luther's shoulder. "I said they *want* me to hide. I didn't say I was going to do it. An old friend of mine is looking for me and I suspect he'll be looking here. So I don't want to disappoint him. There's a little job of work I have to finish."

Sarah came out of the back room then and walked down along the bar to where Ramsey was standing.

"Welcome home, stranger," she said. "We missed seeing your handsome face."

"And do I get a free pint as a welcome home gift?" he said, one hand on her waist.

"A free pint and a big kiss," Sarah said. She put one hand on each side of his face and gave him a soft, quick kiss on the mouth.

MacNeal came out of the terminal director's office and walked over to where Harris was waiting.

"How about the car?" he asked.

"All set," Harris said. "A Citroën and a hard-nosed driver."

"Good. Let's go." They walked quickly across the terminal.

"Did you get the General?" Harris asked.

"I got him all right."

"What's the plan?" Harris said.

"Very simple," MacNeal said. "Stop Gallagher. Any way we can."

"That may not be easy," Harris said as they walked through the doorway and got into the Citroën.

"Then we'll have to do it the hard way," MacNeal said.

In Newcastle, Gallagher's plane landed and stood straining, the wind singing across its metal surfaces as Gallagher and Castor bent forward and pushed their way through the wind gusts to the terminal. They ran through the building and got into the first taxi in the line outside.

Sarah came from behind the bar carrying four steins of ale on a tray. She threaded her way through the crowd to Ramsey's table in the corner. She set the mugs down in front of Ramsey, Luther and the two girls sitting with them.

"Four beers for four dears and a kiss on the cheek for the host," she said, picking up her tray and giving Ramsey a quick kiss as she headed back to the bar.

"She's in good spirits tonight," one of the girls said.

The other girl said, "You don't often see Sarah handin' out kisses to the trade like that."

"I think she's developed a warm spot in her heart for our friend here," Luther said.

"If you ask me," the first girl said, "she's got a warm spot somewhere else."

"That's it, Mary," the second girl said. "That's more the truth of it."

143

"I have only this to say," Ramsey said. "If I'm chosen, I am available."

Far to the southwest of Newcastle, skidding and speeding through a cold and driving rainstorm, MacNeal's car raced through the town of Settle.

"How far now?" MacNeal asked the driver.

"A little over ninety kilometers. The weather's getting worse, too. It'll be slow going from here on."

Inside the Stafford House, Gallagher and Castor followed the bellman into their room, the same room they had taken before. Tipping the man and closing the door behind him, Gallagher went to the window, closed the shades, and looked out around the edge at the Victoria down below. Castor picked up the phone and asked the operator for a number.

A moment later, a barman came out of the back room of the Victoria and walked to the far end of the bar where Sarah stood talking with Ramsey.

"Telephone, Sarah," the barman said. "In the office."

Sarah turned to Ramsey and said, "I'll just be a minute. Meanwhile you'd better go back to your friends or one of those fine ladies might put a hatpin in my heart."

Inside her office she picked up the receiver and said, "Hello." Then, "Oh, just a moment, then." She closed the door and came back to the phone. "Just ask me yes and no questions," she said softly into the mouthpiece. "This place is like a fish bowl."

"Is he there?" Castor asked.

"Yes," she said.

"Does it look as though he'll stay for awhile?"

"Yes," she said.

"We're at the Stafford House. In the same room as before. Are you making progress with him?"

"Yes," she said.

Outside at the bar still, Ramsey looked toward the back room. He left the bar then, walked through the connecting door and tapped on the office door. "Come on, Sarah," he said.

Inside, Sarah said, "Just a second." Then into the phone, "I have to go now."

"All right, Sarah," Castor said. "Call back if you can."

He hung up and walked over to the window where Gallagher stood. "It may be a long wait," he said. "He's there and she says he seems in no hurry to go."

144

"What about the plan?" Gallagher said.

"She says she'll try. But she can't guarantee anything."

Sarah came back into the barroom and walked over to a table where Ramsey was sitting alone. As he put his hand over hers she glanced at the clock behind the bar. Two-thirty.

■ 10 ■

MacNeal's car skidded to a stop at a crossroad. The highway was black and wet but the rain had stopped now. The driver turned a flashlight on the road sign ahead. Newcastle—fifteen kilometers. He put the flashlight on the seat beside him and the car rolled ahead across the intersection.

Gallagher turned his eyes away from the window for a moment. "What time is it?"

"Almost five," Castor said.

"How can she stay open so late?" Gallagher asked.

"She never closes if there's somebody there who wants a drink."

"What about the police?" Gallagher said.

"They look the other way. They'd rather have the roughnecks getting drunk in there because Sarah knows how to handle them. Otherwise they'd be drinking and raising hell all over Newcastle."

After a moment, Gallagher said, "I don't like it, Roy. It's dragging on too long."

"Shall I call her again?" Castor said.

"No," Gallagher said, "you'd better not."

"He can't stay in there forever," Castor said.

"That's right," Gallagher said, "he can't."

Ramsey stood in the back room now, just beside Sarah's office, his arms around her, his body wedging her against the wall.

"Come on, Sarah," he said, "let's go somewhere."

"Just be patient, luv," she said, "in a quarter of an hour my day man'll be in. Then I can leave."

"Come on, Sarah. Let's go now."

"Just a few more minutes and we'll go," she said. "And it's not far to go either. I've got a fine room just across the street."

"Let's go now, Sarah," he whispered.

"Just a few minutes," she said, "and Charlie will be in. It's just across the street, my little place. Second floor of the Stafford House."

"Let's go now, then, sweetheart," he said.

"Just a few more minutes, luv," Sarah said.

In the Bristol railway station, a slovenly fat man, with livid acne scars on his cheeks and neck, shuffled across the waiting area carrying a mop and pail. No trains were scheduled in or out for over an hour and the station was empty. As he came into the men's washroom, he heard a muffled pounding and shouting coming from the utility closet. As he unlocked the door and opened it, the thin man in the tweed hat burst out, pushed the attendant to one side and ran out into the terminal. Behind him, still sitting groggily on the floor of the closet, was the man in the light-colored raincoat, his head in his hands. In the terminal, the man in the tweed hat ran across to a phone booth, slid into it, and slammed the door behind him.

Luther was still sitting at the corner table, smoking a pipe and sipping cognac. The two girls were asleep now, their heads resting on their arms on the smooth wood table top. Ramsey walked over and sat down beside Luther.

"I'll be leaving in a few minutes. Go wait for me at your place."

Luther looked up at Sarah. "Is she the job you said you had to do?" he asked Ramsey.

"No," Ramsey smiled, "this is a new project. That other job can wait till I'm back."

"How long will you be?" Luther asked.

"About an hour. I'll see you at your place."

In Ramsey's apartment, the telephone rang. The gray-haired man who had driven his car earlier got up from a sofa where he had been lying fully dressed, his coat thrown over him, switched on a lamp and hurried to the phone.

"Yes. No. No, he's not. This is Jaycoxe. Yes . . . yes. . . ."

MacNeal's car rolled off the highway and turned into the outskirts of Newcastle.

"This is it," the driver said. "We're at the edge of Newcastle."

"Do you know the water front?" MacNeal asked.

"Yes, sir. It's a little way from here."

"Well, let's get down there," MacNeal said. "Fast."

Inside the Victoria, Sarah, her apron off, moved about quickly now, preparing to leave. She went to her office, then came back to Ramsey. As she came up beside him, the telephone rang faintly in the office behind her.

"Don't answer it," Ramsey said.

Sarah looked at him for a long moment and said, "All right, I won't." She caught the barman's eye and shook her head. The phone rang five more times. Then it stopped. Sarah walked to the back wall, opened a switch box, and pulled the handle. The barroom and the back room and the office went completely dark.

Across the street, Gallagher said, "There go the lights."

Castor walked over to the window and looked out. As they watched the dark building across the way, the lights flickered and came on again. The display sign in front, the colored neon tubes in the window and the inside lights glowing dimly through the glass panes.

"That's the signal," Castor said. "She'll be out in two minutes."

Sarah closed the switch box and walked back toward Ramsey. There were three or four men still at the bar and a dozen or so people still drinking or dozing at the tables.

"What was that all about?" Ramsey asked her.

"You mean the lights?" Sarah said.

"Yes, what's the point of that?"

Sarah said she did it to please the police. "It's a bit of a technicality. They allow me to stay open late but not all night. When the lights went out I closed up. When I turned them on again, I opened up for today."

"Can you leave now?" Ramsey asked.

"Right now," she said, "soon as I get my coat."

"I'll go with you to get it," Ramsey said as she started for the office.

"Come along then," she said.

147

Castor pulled on a heavy peacoat and a wool seaman's cap. Gallagher switched off the lights, then walked to the window and opened the shades wider.

"She said she'd bring him up the back stairs," Castor said. "I'll wait downstairs till they come inside. Then I'll follow along behind them."

"Remember," Gallagher said, "I don't want anybody in here but him and me."

"I think you're wrong about that," Castor said.

"Maybe I am," Gallagher said, "but that's the way it has to be."

"All right," Castor said. "I'll just give him a bit of a shove from the rear to help him through the door." He stepped out into the hallway then, pulling the door shut behind him. Gallagher went back to the window.

Jaycoxe, buttoning his coat, bare-headed, came out of Ramsey's apartment, ran down the stairs to the street and started running toward the water front.

In the back room, Sarah, wearing her coat now, pushed Ramsey gently away from her, touched his cheek with her hand and said, "Come on, then. Let's go home." She took his hand and led him out of the back room toward the front door.

In the street, Castor eased out the side door of the hotel and stood hidden in the shadows a few feet from the entrance.

Gallagher, looking down from the window, saw Castor move into position in the darkness. He looked back down at the entrance to the Victoria. Above the buildings he could see the first streaks of dark light as the night began to break up over the North Sea.

MacNeal's car screeched around the corner, narrowly missed a drunken man staggering along in the grayness, straightened itself, and raced on toward the docks.

Jaycoxe, running down the sidewalk, stepped off the curb at the corner and ran on down the middle of the street toward the Victoria.

Sarah and Ramsey, just inside the front door. The barman

148

who had just come on duty, the day man, came out of the back room and said, "Sarah, excuse me, but could I see you for a second before you leave?"

Sarah looked quickly at Ramsey. He shook his head.

"I'll just be a second," she said, walking to meet the barman. "Yes, Charlie," she said.

A few minutes later, Castor, immobile in the darkness, saw two figures step out through the lighted doorway of the Victoria.

Jaycoxe stumbled, lurched against a parked car, and almost fell. Straightening himself, seeing the silhouette of the Stafford House on down the street, he started to run again.

MacNeal's car turned into the long street leading down to the docks.

Gallagher, his shoulder stiff against the window frame, his eyes fixed on the street below, could see the panorama of the street and buildings and the dark sky slowly breaking up, the city of Newcastle in gloomy silhouette. And dead in the center foreground, two figures, Ramsey and Sarah, their arms around each other, moved forward a few steps from the door. As Gallagher watched, Ramsey pulled her to him and kissed her.

Castor moved back deeper into the shadows as Sarah, laughing and gently pushing Ramsey away from her, pulled him along across the street toward the side entrance of the hotel.

Gallagher, with a cold sickness in his stomach, watched Ramsey, his arms around Sarah, moving slowly forward in the center of the street. Off to the right, a movement caught his eye. A man running, turning the corner of the Victoria, and stopping when he saw Ramsey.

"Norman!" Jaycoxe shouted.

Castor pressed his back tight against the side of the hotel as he tried to fade further into the dimness, as he watched the man walk over to Ramsey and Sarah. The man took Ramsey's arm and pulled him a few steps away from Sarah. They stood with their backs to her, the man talking urgently.

Gallagher, watching, saw Ramsey turn his head away from

the man and look at Sarah who stood waiting where he had left her. He turned back to the man then, the man still talking. Again he turned to look at Sarah. As he looked at her, she edged a step backward toward the hotel entrance, toward Castor hidden there. Ramsey said something to the man, then walked over toward Sarah.

Castor felt the perspiration in the palms of his hands as he watched Ramsey moving slowly forward. Ramsey turned Sarah to him and he seemed to be smiling as he said something to her. Then he swung his arm and hit her in the face. As she bent over to protect herself, he swung his other fist and hit her again.

As Sarah sank down to the ground Gallagher saw Castor come running out from the shadows by the hotel entrance. He grabbed Ramsey by both shoulders and shook him like a padded dummy. Then he sledge-hammered him on the side of the head with his fist and Ramsey fell. As Castor lifted Ramsey from the ground to hit him again, Gallagher saw Jaycoxe pull a gun from his coat and step in behind Castor. As he brought the barrel down on Castor's head, Gallagher was away from the window and into the hallway, heading for the back stairs with his gun in his hand.

Sarah lay on the ground, shaking her head and trying to see clearly, trying to sit up. Out of the blurred grayness she blinked three figures into partial focus. As she shook her head again, she saw Castor face down on the ground and Jaycoxe behind him, helping Ramsey to his feet. Ramsey, shaking his head, too, to clear it, took the gun from Jaycoxe, walked over to Castor and, leaning over, pressed it against the back of his head.

Gallagher, coming out of the side door of the hotel, heard Sarah scream just as he heard the shot. Ramsey was just straightening up over Castor.

"Ramsey!" Gallagher yelled, stepping forward out of the doorway. Ramsey whirled and fired and stepped behind Jaycoxe. Gallagher fired as he felt Ramsey's bullet slam him back against the hotel wall. He fired again and Jaycoxe fell over backward in the street. Ramsey fired again as he backed toward the corner and ran down the long street leading to the docks. The bullet slammed into the hotel wall just over Gallagher's head. Gallagher stood, shaken and sick, against the wall. He watched Ramsey disappear around the corner of the Stafford

House. Then, his left arm hanging straight and heavy at his side, his upper arm torn by the bullet and blood running warmly down inside his sleeve, he pushed himself away from the side of the hotel and started to run after Ramsey.

■ 11 ■

As MacNeal's car pulled up halfway between the Victoria and the Stafford House, as MacNeal and Harris jumped out on either side of the still-rolling car, Ramsey was already a hundred yards away, running southeast on the dock street; Sarah, joined by the barman and all the customers from inside, was kneeling by Castor's body, and Gallagher, his left hand folded across his chest now, his thumb hooked in his shirt front, his gun in the other hand, had turned the corner of the hotel and was running, imperfectly but strongly, along the dock street after Ramsey.

"Jim," MacNeal called. He and Harris, their guns in their hands, ran forward a few steps and stopped, watching Ramsey and Gallagher running down the dock street.

"Stop, Jim," MacNeal shouted. "Don't make me shoot you." "Stop, Jim," he called again a moment later as Gallagher, not looking back, kept running. Stumbling and bent over, but still running, a scattered pattern of blood drops shining in the street behind him.

"He's not gonna stop," Harris said.

"I guess not," MacNeal said. "The crazy bastard." Then, "All right. Let's go." The two men started running down the dark street, Gallagher now a hundred staggering yards ahead, Ramsey over two hundred yards and nearly out of sight sometimes behind the crates and oil drums and bales and boxes stacked at points along the wharfside.

Ramsey, looking over his shoulder now, seeing three men coming instead of one, turned sharply and started up the gangplank of a rusting tanker. An old sailor, a watchman with a white mustache, appeared suddenly at the top of the gangplank, his hands in his peacoat pockets. Ramsey stopped,

151

hesitated a second, then ran back down the gangplank and on up the street along the wharves.

MacNeal and Harris were gaining ground now on Gallagher. Harris stopped suddenly then, and MacNeal, running on past, raised his gun and fired. Gallagher, hit on the left side again, this time high in the shoulder, pitched forward and fell face down in the street.

MacNeal stopped short and stood looking ahead at Gallagher struggling to get up as Harris, running again, passed him and a few yards further on, stopped and raised his gun to fire again. Gallagher was on his knees now, facing backward, raising his gun slowly.

"Harris!" MacNeal called. "Wait."

Gallagher fired and Harris, his gun still raised, spurted blood from a hole under his cheekbone. He slumped to his knees, then went down heavily on his side.

MacNeal ran to kneel over Harris and turn him over, to see his wide-open dead eyes as Gallagher, with a push from his right hand, pushing hard against the ground, straightened himself up into a crouch and ran on up the street in a shambling stagger.

MacNeal stood up now and looked after the stumbling, still running Gallagher. Then he started forward again, walking now, his hand holding his gun straight down at his side.

Ramsey stopped again now beside another tanker, a dilapidated gangway stretching from the wharf to its deck. His eyes swept along from the bow to the stern. He saw no one. No sign of life. As he started up the gangway, Gallagher lurched to a stop thirty yards back, raised his gun and fired. The bullet sang past Ramsey's head and spanged against the side of the ship, sending chunks and splinters of rust flying and falling in an orange spray to the water. Ramsey fired a shot toward Gallagher, raced on up the gangway and disappeared behind the wheelhouse among the empty cases and barrels and oil drums on the deck.

Gallagher, unable to run now, moved forward in a loping, lopsided walk, his right hand holding the gun and squeezing the bicep of his throbbing left arm. The blood was soaked through his outer coat now. Long dark stains on his left sleeve. And oozing through in the back, high on his left shoulder. He muttered to himself as he dragged himself forward, "Hang on. Hang on."

At the foot of the gangplank, he dropped behind a packing

crate, slumped to his knees, bent over, his head down. Slowly, painfully, his breath coming in raw gulps, he raised his head, crawled forward to the edge of the crate and looked up the gangway to the deck. No movement. He looked back toward MacNeal. He was walking steadily forward. Still fifty yards away. Gallagher looked back toward the deck of the ship. Still no life there. He hooked his right hand over the top of the crate and pulled himself up. "Hang on." Half-crouching, half-standing, he looked again toward the deck. He saw nothing. In a loose, crazy, sidewise run, he started up the gangplank. Half-way up a shot came from the left of the wheelhouse and ricocheted off a rail post of the gangway. Leaning against the post, Gallagher fired a shot back at Ramsey and saw his head duck down behind an oil drum. Gallagher lurched on up the gangway then, winging off another shot and hearing it spang off the oil drum.

Ramsey crawled quickly across to another obstruction, an empty machinery crate, rose up suddenly and fired just as Gallagher reached the top of the gangway and started across the deck.

Gallagher, blood squirting from his right thigh, fell to the deck and dragged himself behind the wheelhouse opposite the side where Ramsey was barricaded. With a last shudder of strength he crawled into a cluster of boxes and barrels and sat there, leaning against them, facing out, his right hand pressing hard against the artery in his thigh, his head back, his face gray against the wall of barrels and cases. Muttering to himself weakly, "My God. My God."

Behind his barricade on the other side, Ramsey crouched and waited and listened. He heard a sound at the foot of the gangway and, as he turned his head, he saw MacNeal drop out of sight behind the box where Gallagher had hidden a moment before.

MacNeal squatted there. He checked his gun and listened. He eased forward and looked up the gangway. Nothing. He raised himself up for a better look. Still nothing. "Ramsey," MacNeal called. He crouched down, waiting. There was no answer. "Ramsey," he called again. Then he waited again. The sky was getting much lighter now. There was a tiny stripe of pink-orange at the horizon line out to the east, out across the harbor mouth toward the North Sea. "Stay down and hold your fire, Ramsey. I'm coming aboard but I'm not after you."

He hunched down waiting. There was no movement on the

ship and no sound. No answer. "I'm coming aboard now, Ramsey."

Slowly, MacNeal rose to a crouch, his head over the top of his barricade, his eyes scanning the deck. He moved slowly to his right and, easily, watching, he started up the gangplank. One easy deliberate step at a time. Listening and watching. One slow step after another up to the top of the gangway. Up to the deck. He paused there for a half-breath, then dived to the deck and rolled to the bulkhead of the wheelhouse. Slowly he pulled his legs under him then in a crouching knee-bend, his back hard against the bulkhead, his gun in front of him, his eyes taking in the deck. Ahead of him, trailing off slightly forward and to his left was a smudged trail of blood with a few bright drops beside it on the worn boards of the deck. "Stay down, Ramsey. I'm not after you," he called again. There was no answer. No sound. Slowly MacNeal moved forward after the smeared trail of blood, moving in a knee-bent crouch, duck-waddling across the deck.

Gallagher, his gun beside him on the deck, his hand still pressed hard, but weaker now, against that pumping artery inside his thigh, looked up at MacNeal as he crawled around a box and into the U-shaped cave where Gallagher sat. MacNeal squatted five feet away from him, his gun in his hand, taking in Gallagher's face like ashes, the limp sprawl of his legs, the gun on the deck. Gallagher breathing heavily with blood oozing from his shoulder and from his arm and threatening to spurt his life away in seconds if he loosened the pressure on his thigh with his hand. But his eyes burned hot out of the grayness of his face and locked with MacNeal's eyes. For a long frozen moment, they stared at each other without moving. Then MacNeal put his own gun in his pocket and crept forward, pulling the belt off his coat as he went. He slipped it under Gallagher's leg, bound it twice around high on his thigh and pulled it tighter and tighter and into a blood-stopping knot. Gallagher's eyes never left him as he quickly made the tourniquet and as MacNeal edged back, the belt strapped tightly in place, Gallagher stared into his eyes, a look like a weapon. "You crazy son of a bitch," MacNeal said. But his eyes stayed with Gallagher's, a contact like a vine connecting two trees.

Ramsey, listening and watching, heard nothing. He edged forward to look. He crawled forward until he could look along the deck to the other side of the wheelhouse. There was no sound or movement there.

"MacNeal!" he called. Then, when there was no answer, "MacNeal, if you don't want me to start shooting, you'd better answer."

MacNeal crawled away from Gallagher to the edge of the barricade. "Yeah!" he called.

"What's happening over there?" Ramsey yelled.

"Nothing. Gallagher's shot."

"Is he dead?"

"No," MacNeal said, "but he can't move."

"What if I don't believe you?"

"Then come over and look for yourself."

After a moment, Ramsey said, "I don't think that's such a good idea. Why don't you stroll over here. Then we'll go look at Gallagher together." No answer. "Well, how about it?"

MacNeal turned back to look at Gallagher again, still in the same position, sprawled, propped up, looking back at him. "All right," MacNeal called. Then to Gallagher, "I've got to do it, Jim."

"Good," Ramsey called. "Come on over then. Nice and easy." He crawled back behind the oil drums where he had first barricaded himself, behind a stack of rusting and oil-stained metal drums. "I'm waiting," he called. "Are you coming?"

MacNeal bent over and picked up Gallagher's gun from the deck. Standing over him, with the gun in his hand, he said again, "I've got to do it, Jim." Then, holding the gun at his side, he backed away, turned and walked away from Gallagher, around the wheelhouse toward Ramsey. His face was lined and expressionless as he walked, his eyes cold and gray.

"All right," Ramsey said, rising up, "stop right there." He studied MacNeal carefully as he stood there, fifteen feet away, his coat open, his face pale and tired, his arms straight down at his sides, his crisp gray hair blowing in the predawn air blowing in off the ocean. "Very good, Mr. MacNeal. Very good so far. Now, if you'll just toss that revolver to me." Then, "Go ahead. Toss it here."

MacNeal brought his arm up in an easy motion and tossed the gun across the oil drums to Ramsey, who slipped it into his own coat pocket, keeping his eyes on MacNeal's face as he stood facing him.

"Now," Ramsey said, "put your hands in your coat pockets and keep them there. That's it. Now walk over here to where I am."

MacNeal walked slowly forward and as he came around

155

behind Ramsey's shelter, Ramsey eased slowly backward, keeping a distance of about ten feet between them.

"That's good," Ramsey said. "Stop right there." Then, "You say Gallagher can't move?"

"That's right," MacNeal said.

"I know I hit him twice, so you're probably telling the truth. At least I can afford to trust you for a moment or two. Then I'll go over and look for myself."

"He can't move," MacNeal said. "He's lost a lot of blood."

Ramsey studied MacNeal for a long moment. Then he said, "For the last few days I've been getting reports that a man named MacNeal had arrived in England from Washington. My people even managed to show me a photograph of you. Then last evening in Liverpool, I got word that this Mr. MacNeal was anxious to talk to me. Is that true?"

"Yes," MacNeal said. "It's important."

"All right," Ramsey said, "you wait here for one moment while I go take a look at Gallagher, then I'll take you someplace where we can chat." Off up toward the city, a police siren sounded very faintly. "Yes, I think we should definitely get away from here for our little talk." Ramsey circled around MacNeal, crab-walking to his right, keeping a ten-foot distance. "On second thought, you'd better follow along behind me. That's it. Nice and easy. We'll be away from here in less than a minute." Ramsey backed slowly along the deck. MacNeal behind him.

"Why don't you leave Gallagher the way he is?" MacNeal said. "I told you he's helpless. He can't hurt you."

Ramsey smiled, still backing away, getting close to the other side of the wheelhouse now. "It's a matter of principle, Mr. MacNeal. I've botched this job twice before. I can't let that happen again. You might say my honor is at stake."

Ramsey, still backing up, looked quickly over his right shoulder and saw Gallagher sitting where MacNeal had left him. His eyes wide open still and staring, not at Ramsey, but past him at MacNeal.

Ramsey stopped at Gallagher's feet and motioned MacNeal to a stop a few feet away. Ramsey looked down at Gallagher then. Missing nothing. The three wounds, the limp body propped up, the hands loose and palms up on the deck.

"You were right," Ramsey said to MacNeal. "He's helpless but he's not dead."

156

MacNeal, pinned like a moth by Gallagher's eyes, said, "He doesn't have to be dead. You don't have to kill him."

The siren sounded closer now. Coming from the center of town. Not at the water front yet. But getting closer.

"Oh, yes, I do," Ramsey said. "As I said, it's a point of honor with me. You might even call it survival. Also," he smiled at MacNeal as he brought his gun up, pointing it at Gallagher's chest, "also, I suspect that once Jimbo is dead, you'll suddenly decide that you have nothing to talk to me about after all."

"I don't know what you mean by that," MacNeal said.

"Yes, you do, MacNeal. You know exactly what I mean."

MacNeal, looking at Ramsey's smooth and confident face, feeling Gallagher's eyes on him still, never wavering in their gaze, clenched his fists tightly in his coat pockets. And somewhere inside him, an ice floe broke slowly away from the mainland and began to float.

"Don't kill him, Ramsey," MacNeal said.

Ramsey, looking down at Gallagher, did not answer or look at MacNeal. Now at last, Gallagher turned his eyes away from MacNeal and looked full up into Ramsey's face, into those clear-blue, innocent eyes. As their eyes met for the first time in all those months since Berlin, as the electricity of those months crackled back and forth between them, the first shot slammed its shocking sound into their ears. Followed by two more, close together and raw in the morning silence.

Ramsey and Gallagher still looked at each other for an agonizing frozen moment. Then Ramsey broke and sagged back against a barrel, his gun arm dropping straight down and a bullet firing into the deck beside Gallagher. Looking quickly then at MacNeal, Gallagher saw him step forward toward Ramsey. As Gallagher watched, MacNeal fired three more times through his coat pocket. Three more point-blank bullets burned through the cloth and thumped into Ramsey.

Ramsey, thrown back against the barrels and packing cases, stretched up slowly to his full height, as though beginning a magnificent stretching yawn, then stiffened suddenly, that boyish, cricket-player smile frozen across his mouth, and fell straight forward to the deck, just at Gallagher's feet. Like the bar of a crucifix across the column of Gallagher's legs.

The police car and an ambulance screeched to a stop on the dock street beside the tanker. As four policemen and three ambulance attendants ran up the gangway to the deck, MacNeal turned away from Gallagher and walked to meet them. And as the attendants with a stretcher and their instruments in black bags hurried toward him across the deck, Gallagher at last let his eyes close.

In the ambulance, as it backed away from the exit of the wharf to turn around and head for the city, Gallagher opened his eyes again. MacNeal was there beside the ambulance bed. Bent over beside the bed talking with one of the doctors. When Gallagher closed his eyes this time he went to sleep. His breathing was slow and regular and his heartbeat was steady as the ambulance raced through the streets of Newcastle with its siren wailing.

Over the bed, above Gallagher's body, from the bottles hanging on a rack there, liquid dripped steadily down the clear plastic tubes and into his veins.

Keep Up With The BESTSELLERS!